Treacle Town

Leigh Dyson

ISBN: 9798746681393

It's the address no one aspires to.
Treacle Town.

It's the start in life no one needs.
Abandoned at birth.
Given away as a baby.

It's the cv no one employs.
Taught to thieve as a child.
Trained to kill as a youth.

It's the reputation no one wants.
The Devils Whelp.

But when you live with it you have to limit your ambition.
Or do you?

Chapter One

Sunday 11th July 1897

'Who will take this child of the Parish?'

The tiny baby was wrapped in a white swaddling blanket as Reverend Popplewell held it chest high, pushing his arms out towards the congregation. His flock were dressed in their Sunday best, all sitting dutifully in their pews. The well to do, who donated generously to church funds, sat at the front in their reserved places. Behind them came the volunteers, the ladies who ran the tea mornings and fund-raising fetes sitting alongside their husbands. Finally, the majority of churchgoers, both the ones who came in regularly and the erratic worshipers who sat at the back.

Normally at this point in the service all eyes were focused upon the Reverend as he gave his sermon, his words of wisdom for the week. But not today, this was the third Sunday in a row he had offered the child to his parishioners and, as on both previous occasions, he was met by silence, downcast eyes and turned shoulders. No one wanted the new-borne babe. Popplewell was both disappointed and understanding, but the child had to go. The woman feeding it wanted no more and he could not tend for it. A strained silence reigned, shuffles, snuffles and coughs all halted in case they were misinterpreted as interest.

Popplewell was at a loss, nothing had prepared him for this, he had tried his best, appealing to Christian charity and the kind caring hearts of the Parish, for surely in this the year of our Lord 1897 the community would not cast a babe into the wilderness. Even when Albert Cadman and Percy Shaw each gave a charitable donation of forty shillings towards its fostering and Popplewell added ten shillings from the Church funds, even then, none of his Parishioners

5

would take it. If he failed here today, he knew he faced a difficult talk with the bishop trying to explain why the Parish of Wath could not look after its own and why a Church, somewhere else, should take the child in.

It was a boy he held in his arms, a boy found abandoned before the Sunday Service three weeks ago, covered only in a tatty sheet on a grave stone in the Churchyard. The problem was not the baby, it was the grave stone. It was the grave of Abel Dyson, father of the murderer Edwin Dyson. The younger Dyson had been hanged in York just five weeks past for the vicious murder of three men, men he claimed assaulted his young wife, Coleen. A claim the Judge deemed irrelevant to his crime. The verdict of guilty was inevitable as Dyson did not protest his innocence but, combined with the level of violence involved, the failure of his wife to appear in court to back his claim and his lack of remorse the sentence was to be hung by the neck until dead.

Now there were three faces missing from the pews, women were sitting closer to one another than they had six months ago and the heavy weight resting over the top of the congregation since the murders was yet to be lifted.

Neither Dyson nor his wife had been churchgoers, he was an insignificant man the Reverend could hardly remember, but she was different. A stunning looking woman with a self-assured air and a quick and memorable laugh, she stood out on the street or in the shop or anywhere he saw her. She was a woman who everyone noticed. Since the verdict he often wondered why she had not been to court to defend her husband but she had not been seen since his arrest and, it was assumed, she had gone home to her native Ireland.

Regardless, malicious rumours spread that she had returned in secret and left the child as Edwin's revenge. For, ahead of his hanging, Edwin Dyson had sworn a death oath to avenge himself upon the folk of Wath upon Dearne, the folk who he said abandoned him in his hour of need, the folk who turned their backs as he begged for help. The folk, thought Popplewell, who were now

6

refusing to give shelter to a helpless child because of a grave stone, ridiculous rumours and naïve petty-minded superstitions.

But in his death speech Edwin Dyson had cussed them loud and long, uttering profanity after profanity as he stood with the noose around his neck. He cursed the people who did nothing to stop the attacks on him and his wife, pledged he would return from beyond the grave and promised the people of Wath hardship and pain.

Now a child abandoned on the grave of a murderer's father, a babe of no more than a few hours when abandoned, a child offered up to God's mercy, was being shunned by a reluctant congregation. They were cowed by the words of a man who no longer existed, a man who would surely be turned away from eternal happiness, suffering himself the miseries he plotted for others; for eternity.

Just as his hopes of a successful outcome for the child evaporated Popplewell became aware of a stirring at the back of the Church, a young couple stood up, the woman stepping into the aisle pulling the man behind her. Both looked shy and over awed as they moved forward. Popplewell was certain he had never seen them before and sighed as they moved up the aisle enabling him to see them more clearly. She had a tear in her dress, they were both unkempt and grimy, they were not regular members of his flock, they were boat people.

The Don and Dearne Canal ran through the centre of Wath upon Dearne and it had once been a major thoroughfare for barges carrying coal from the pits in the area but now the railways were in full flow and the barge operators had to scrape a living as best they could.

They lived in their boats in appalling conditions, cramped, damp and prone to illness and rat infestations. They never stayed long in one place and were rarely recorded in censuses, tax lists or Church records. Violence and lawlessness followed them as inevitably as horse droppings followed behind a cart. Their children rarely attended school, they were feral, frequenting the bottle returns, cloth merchants and scrap metal dealers like mice in a grain store. They plundered the canal banks and surrounding area as they passed, stealing whatever they could pick up and they were not averse to robbing their own.

Justice was their own to give in a moral code which had few rules or standards and now two of them were walking down the aisle, probably for the first time thought Popplewell, walking towards him as he held the child up high.

He smiled as he passed the child to the woman who upon closer inspection was not unattractive though the effect was destroyed when she opened her mouth. Protruding teeth were stained black and yellow with several gaps, while her breath made him take an involuntary step backward. Gathering himself he leant toward the woman passing the child as he said. 'Thank you my dear, God bless you.'

He could feel the relief surge through his body and was immediately ashamed. This was not what he hoped for. He dreamt of a comfortable home full of love and smiles for the young child, who had hardly made a murmur during the three weeks he had been at the Vicarage. With the help of a wet nurse his housekeeper had reluctantly looked after the baby and he knew they would both be relieved. But there was a tremor in Popplewells voice, a sense of shame that his flock, his people, could not see fit to offer charity to an abandoned baby. He would never be able to look at them in the same light. The people who every Sunday espoused Christian values were abandoning them on mass.

He raised his eyes to the man standing behind the woman. He was older than the woman, thin and wiry with a receding hair line battling wild wispy hair. His red rimmed eyes were over large as the drama of the scene intimidated him. He held a cap in his hands which he crushed and twisted in embarrassment at being in front of so many people. His boots were worn and scuffed, above them canvas strips were wrapped around his shins and calves as leg bindings while his trousers had patches on the knees. A collarless shirt of an indeterminable colour cringed under a waist coat and

8

jacket which were obviously too large for him and probably rescued from some second-hand cloth merchant.

For a fleeting second Popplewell hesitated, could he really give this helpless child to these people. As quickly as the thought entered, he banished it. The child had to go, it was not his fault his congregation had absolved themselves of their charitable nature, neither was it his responsibility to vet the moral disposition of the couple who stepped forward, they were church going Christians - that was enough. His job was to stand here, offer the child and pass him over to whoever stood up. That was all. He could not back down.

He pulled back the blanket wrapping the child, smiled into his face then said to the woman 'Could you please wait until the service is over and I will bring you his things.'

The woman bobbed 'Yes Father.' And, as the man placed a protective arm around her shoulders, proudly carrying the baby, they made their way back to their bench at the back of the Church.

With the Service over Popplewell positioned himself by the collection box at the exit as the Parishioners left, thanking them for their generosity when they made a donation, spearing those who didn't with a glare while maintaining a fixed smile on his lips. After the last moved through the door he turned to the couple still seated at the back of the church. 'One moment please' He walked through to the small ante room behind the font and collected the basket containing the clothes donated by his Ladies tea morning. It was the basket the child had been sleeping in and as the woman placed him inside the familiar surroundings he settled comfortably. The Reverend then took a cloth purse from inside his jacket and passed it to the woman. 'Here is a contribution towards his up keep from our congregation.' The woman thanked him and handed it to the man who grabbed it greedily, not embarrassed to open it and count the money in front of the Vicar. A leering smile crossed his lips.

'Aye, thanks your 'onour, we'd best be goin.'

9

'What about a name?' asked the woman.

'He has not been named as yet' said Popplewell 'perhaps when you do name him you will come back and allow me to baptise him.'

'Aye, course we will your 'onour, but we gotta go.'

'Wait.' said the woman 'where was he found. He has to have a name that means something.'

'What about your name? suggested the Reverend surprised that this was not obvious.

'Don't like it' she said emphatically 'and he ain't aving is!' she gestured vigorously at the man.

'He was found in the churchyard, abandoned on a grave.'

'Who's grave?

'Abel Dyson's.'

'That's it then he's a Dyson from Wath. Wath Dyson.'

'We don't know that for certain my d—.'

'No, but it'll do for now. Cum on, let's go.' interrupted the man grabbing the woman by the arm and dragging her through the door.

Popplewell watched the couple leave the church. He stood in the doorway as they walked up the path. Wath upon Dearne was recorded in the Doomsday book as Waith, a Viking word for wading point or ford. As time evolved a farming hamlet grew on the hill at the side of the bend in the river, the bend, known later as the wash, was, where in times of flood, the waters overflowed into the marshes. Probably through spelling errors, the name morphed to Wath upon Dearne, still holding the pronunciation of the a as in wash. Then with the discovery of coal in the area a canal was built and the wash was put to use. A huge basin was constructed, known locally as the Bay of Biscay, and it was here that passing barges turned or moored when resting. To get back to their boat the couple would turn right out of the churchyard then go down the hill past the old disused prison until they reached the canal.

Popplewell was concerned, the look on the man's face did not give him comfort. The way he clutched the money and shuffled from foot to foot in agitation as the woman spoke to him was worrying. If they turned left out of the Church gates, they would go into Wath upon Dearne itself. Being Sunday, all the shops were shut, the only establishment that was open was the Saracens Head public house. If they turned left that was the only place they could be going, he could not go after them, everyone had seen him give them the child. Popplewell held his breath, please you two, please go home, please turn right.

They turned left.

Monday 16/2/1920

It was a scene from Dante's inferno. Huge slabs of molten earth burning red and orange falling out of the oven retort. Dark smoke billowing from the liquefied slabs raced into the sky in thick black plumes. The glowing red mass slumped, folding itself into contorted shapes as it slid down the embankment, landing in solid iron wagons with a sputtering thud.

Dyson stood swaying as the carriage swung around the corner allowing him to see across the tracks to the front of the set of iron wagons as they were pulled under the drenching tower. Tonnes of water cascaded down onto the fiery magna and in a sizzling cacophony huge clouds of steam rose hiding the firestorm as the vibrant red mass turned into a dull grey pile of valuable saleable coke. At the edge of the steaming pile veils of black dust, aggravated by the gusts caused by the updraught of hot air and steam, flew into the air accompanying the sulphurous fumes belching from the hellhole producing an acrid throat constricting perfume. It was the scent of home.

He could feel the heat of the coke ovens through the carriage windows of the train he was on. Much to the silent disgust of the two other passengers in the carriage he had opened the window and the putrid smell flowed in along with dirt and dust.

The train rocked gently as it crossed the points leading away from Manvers Main Colliery and the coke retorts alongside. Dyson

11

kept his gaze firmly on the way ahead. Two hundred yards later they passed a small row of seven terraced houses.

Treacle Town.

Grim, unloved and lonely, an island of desperate humanity surrounded by railway tracks. Home.

The train was still moving at a snail's pace, its next stop, Wath Central Station, was only a few hundred yards ahead. Dyson peered, trying to see into the houses as they passed, seeking any sign of life in the terrace. But from this side all he could see was a door and window on the ground floor depicting each individual terrace with a bedroom window above. The yard was on the far side of the terrace and if anybody was walking to the outside toilet or feeding the chickens in the communal run, they would be on that side not this.

Undeterred he kept up his vigil, focusing on the end terrace, the house he had called home for ten years even though he had been absent for the last four. There was nothing to see, nothing had changed, the familiar red bricks even the paint hanging off the door looked the same. On the other side of the rails a signal box guarding the passing point over the tracks marked the end of the row of houses. When the terrace fell from view, he reached up and pulled his kit bag from the overhead webbing, setting it at his feet as he waited by the door.

The train lurched to a halt. He pulled the window fully down, leant out and opened the door, stepping onto the platform of Wath Central Station. He was the only passenger to disembark, none were waiting to climb aboard and no one was waiting to greet him. The days of soldiers returning from the war being greeted by bunting, crowds and cheers was long gone.

He stood patiently rolling a cigarette as the Station Master, posing in his splendid outfit, topped off with a matching face mask covering his nose and mouth, dramatically waved a red flag in a flamboyant instruction to the driver. Taking his cue from the signal the driver engaged the engine and with more plumes of steam and smoke the train pulled away from the station.

Dyson watched the scene clear and the pit head gear for Wath Main materialise through the dissipating haze. He studied it for a moment then lit his cigarette. The Station Master marched towards him.

'Mask! Put your mask on. Don't you know there's a bloody pandemic or don't you care!' he yelled at Dyson.

Dyson simply stared at him and pulled once more on his cigarette. It was Saul Smalley. Smalley was two years older than him and had been a shrimp of a boy growing up. But here he was, draped in civilian authority, spewing orders to the people who paid his wages – passengers – like a roman emperor ordering execution at the colosseum.

Dyson didn't move, just waited.

Smalley stopped several yards away waving his arms in frustration. 'You wait, you wait, I'll get the police, then you won't be so cocky in your bloody uniform, War's over don't you know and' waving at the Station rooms, 'don't think you're coming through here because you are not… until you put a mask on.'

Still Dyson waited without saying a word. He flicked the butt of his cigarette onto the empty railway lines and picked up his kit bag. Smalley sucked in breath and pulled himself as tall as he could.

Dyson shouldered his bag, gave Smalley a smouldering look of contempt and turned from him. He stepped off the platform and started to walk alongside the railway lines back down the track the train had just arrived on.

He could sense the recognition creeping through Smalley. Few people would walk down the track. He heard the dawn of understanding in his voice 'Wath? Wath, is that you?'

He ignored him and strode purposefully alongside the metal rails.

Chapter Two

Monday 16/2/1920

Wath Dyson dropped his kit bag on the floor outside the end
terrace and looked back at the other houses. Four were boarded up,
corrugated sheets nailed across the windows and doors, otherwise
the terrace and its yard were exactly as he remembered it. Dusty, run
down and poor.

Originally called Lower Common Lane this was Treacle Town -
a place named by accident, a row of seven terraced houses doomed
by progress. Thrown up to house workers to the newly constructed
glass factory and soap works almost as soon as the terrace was
completed steam locomotion became the vogue and railway lines
were built connecting the Collieries. Built without any thought for
the residents they cut the terrace off from the rest of Wath upon
Dearne. Then more railways were developed connecting North and
South, East and West and the terrace became an island in a sea of
railway tracks.

The first sloppily constructed tracks, made of pig iron rather than
steel, could not take the increased volume of traffic and collapsed
derailing a full set of wagons containing molasses, spilling their
contents onto the terrace. Drowned in tonnes of the syrup, the place
stank sickly sweet for months and the stranded terrace became
known as Treacle Town.

Then the pits needed sidings to store coal wagons ready for
onward travel and yet more lines surrounded Treacle Town. Still the
pits needed more space and they eyed the terrace greedily but it did
not surrender. Desperate people with nowhere else to go gravitated
to it, gave it life, but were despised and shunned by the rest of Wath
upon Dearne. It was a refugee camp in all but name. And when the

time came that Wath and his mother found themselves cast adrift from their boat they came ashore here.

Treacle Town became home.

He lifted the latch on the door to the end terrace and pushed it open. No one locked their doors, there was little to steal. He called 'hello' as he shouldered his way in and looked around the kitchen. There was no fire, it felt colder inside than out, pots were stacked at the sink and there was a layer of dust on the table. There were some clothes, a couple of thread bare towels on the floor and the cellar door was open. It all had the smell of decay and neglect.

He pushed through to the front room, there was a layer of dust covering everything and an even deeper air of desertion. Climbing the stairs, he looked into his old bedroom, apart from a bed without a mattress, its bed springs dull and rusty, the room was empty.

Opening the door to the cupboard above the stairs he saw his old clothes, still stacked as he had left them. Lucy's clothes were noticeably absent.

He stepped across the landing and looked into his mother's bedroom. Clothes were strewn across the floor and the bed sheets were scrunched up in a pile in the centre of the bed. Wath stood and looked for a long time, his mother had lived most of her life on boats where, in tiny cramped conditions, tidiness was a necessity. Scattered clothes were wrong.

Returning down the stairs and stepping outside he grabbed his kit bag, threw it into the kitchen then walked the few yards past a boarded-up terrace to the next working door. He hammered on the wood.

'Jimmy, you there?' he shouted.

For a long time, there was no answer then a weak voice croaked back.

'Don't come in. I got it, the flu.' a hacking cough exploded after the effort of talking and consumed the speaker for a long minute. Wath waited patiently. When the hacking had subsided, he called again.

15

'Jimmy. It's Wath. you okay, can I help?'

Another long wait ensued as a coughing fit over took the occupant again.

'Wath is that really you?'

'Aye, it be.' he said to the door.

'Stay away Wath, I got the bug.'

'Okay, but can I help?'

'No. Stay away.'

Wath stood looking at the door uncertain as what to do. After a few seconds he turned and went back into the terrace yard. Jimmy was a hard man, a miner for twenty years he knew how to look after himself, if he said to stay away then he would go.

He walked to the only other unboarded door in the terrace and banged. There was no reply. After a full minute banging and waiting he moved out of the yard looking up at the signal box. Believing he recognised the figure inside he climbed the wooden steps and rapped on the glass panel in the wood framed door. Frank Salkeld waved at him and gestured for him to enter.

'Took your time coming back, dint you.'

'Aye' he replied perching on the window sill. He pulled out his makings and started to roll a cigarette. He gestured to Frank *want one?* Frank shook his head. A comfortable quiet ensued as two men used to each-others company waited for the other to speak. It was Frank who broke the silence.

'Want a brew?'

'Love one.'

The signal box was a long thin wooden building with steps leading up to the first floor where windows gave views on three sides. Most of the middle of the windowless far wall held a bank of levers with a panel above. Each lever controlled one set of points with either an off or on position and a brake handle to hold it in place. The panel above had holes cut into it revealing different coloured flags connected by painted lines in a mock-up of the rail track they controlled. Frank moved across to the table and sink

16

where a pot-bellied stove had a kettle simmering on its hob. As he spooned leaves into the tea pot a bell rang out three times. On the display which dominated the long wall a green flag inside one hole turned red.

Wath stood up and looked at Frank.

'Number nineteen, open and hold?'

'Aye' said Frank watching in surprise as Wath went straight to the correct lever, let go the brake, pushed the lever into the open position before reconnecting the brake mechanism. The flag inside the hole moved again, this time tuning green. It was at least four years since Wath had been inside the signal box but he had not forgotten.

Frank recalled the days when a young lad, bright with enthusiasm and new to Treacle Town, spent hours inside the box keeping him company and usually doing most of the work. Wath had been fascinated by the workings of the signals and points and questioned the operators mercilessly. By the time he left for the war, he probably knew the system better than all the men who worked there combined.

As he pulled the lever Frank noted the sleeve of his uniform. There was an unmistakable scar in the material on the upper arm where something had been ripped off. It could only be insignia. Frank wondered what rank he had aspired to and why there was no insignia now. The lad would tell him when he was ready, no rush. Wath turned to face him.

'What happened Frank?'

'To what? he replied. A lot happens in four years.

'Mam.'

'Flu.' Answered Frank bluntly. There was no point dressing anything up, he had seen the lad go into the yard, watched him enter the house, he would have guessed by now. 'Two weeks ago, give a day or two, nobody really knew how long she'd been lying there.'

Wath took a long pull on his cigarette, accepted the mug of tea with a nod and looked out of the window. Another retort was being discharged and black clouds billowed around a glowing red mass. The smoke twirled around itself forming a vortex and started the journey down the railway line. It would reach them in a few seconds and they would hold their breath rather than suck the poison, tar and grime into their lungs. When it had passed Wath pressed for more.

'Lucy?'

Frank sighed he had guessed this question was coming. 'She tried her best lad but the death of young Arthur unhinged her. She had no idea if you would come back. So many boys didn't and he… well he just kept at her day after day. Eventually she started walking out with him, leaving Alice with your mother. And then… well… then taking Alice she upped and left. Moved in with him.'

There was a long period of quiet as Wath absorbed the information. It was little more than he already knew but Frank was a good man, dependable, they had a bond many years in the making and he was one of the few men Wath trusted unconditionally. He sighed, surprised at the lack of feeling. He had thought that coming back would intensify the pain, reopen the wound, resurrect the anguish that had ripped through him, anguish which had settled uncomfortably deep inside his bone marrow. He stood up.

'Thanks for the tea.'

As he reached the door Frank added 'Good to see you lad, glad you got back.'

'Aye.' Wath descended the stairs but at the bottom stopped, changed his mind and retraced his steps. Standing in the door frame, holding the door open he asked.

'What about the Jenkinson's? Are they ok?'

'As far as I know, why?'

'Not answering their door.'

'Be out. Try tomorrow, if they don't answer, give me a knock and we'll check together.'

Wath nodded, descended the steps and this time walked home.

Back inside he picked up the clothes from the floor and used the towels to wipe down the armchair, table, chairs and sink. He ran the tap until the water turned clear from the rust speckled black that first fell into the sink. Pulling back the cloth that hung under the sink as a door to the shelves behind, he found a kettle. Then he went down the cellar, there was a small pile of coal and a bucket. He filled the bucket and checked the tins and cans on the shelves at the top of the cellar stairs. One contained tea which he took into the kitchen. Using the coals from the cellar he lit a fire and started to boil water.

Once he had a steaming mug of tea and the fire was roaring, he went upstairs and emptied the cupboard containing his clothes. Surprisingly moths hadn't bothered them and he took them downstairs. Trousers, shirts, a waistcoat, and two jackets. Memories flooded back as he lay them over the back of a chair but, with an iron will the army would have been proud of, he pushed them to one side. He stripped and tried the clothes on, they were baggy in a few places but overall, they were still serviceable.

Checking every pocket in his uniform, he lined his money up on the table alongside three paper cuttings. Seventeen shillings and six pennies.

His total worth after four years away.

Undeterred he emptied his kit bag putting useful items such as his water bottle, belt and blanket on the table. His underwear, socks and boots joined them. The rest he piled up in front of the fire. Finally, he took his dress jacket and slowly removed the medals from the breast pocket placing them alongside his money on the table.

Then settling himself comfortably in front of the fire he began to burn the individual items of his uniform one by one. Waiting in a trance like state until each had burned to cinders the action became a ritual, a purging. With each item he made a solemn promise never to go back, to never think about that part of his life.

19

Long into the night he watched as every piece joined the smoke from Manvers and four years of his life was consigned to the past.

It was over.

Chapter Three

The next morning, refreshed from a night sleeping wrapped in his blanket in the armchair in front of the fire, he walked out of Treacle Town down the track towards Manvers. Standing behind one of the signals he waited until a Midland mainline train came past, slowing to a crawl as it navigated the points around the tight bend known as the Colliery Curve. As it trundled by, he trotted out, grabbed the handrail, pulled himself up and sat on the footwell of the last carriage. Getting himself comfortable he smoked a cigarette and watched the familiar landscape unfold.

Twenty minutes later as the train crossed the bridge over the River Don and slowed to enter Doncaster Station he jumped down and walked into the town centre. After half an hour of walking the streets, he chose Winfield and Son, pushing the door to the Pawnbrokers open. A door at the back of the counter opened and a young woman set one foot into the room before stopping and spitting the word 'mask!' at him.

'Not got one' he replied ignoring her look of absolute disgust 'ask him if he wants to buy these.' He said pointing at the shelves on the back wall and placing a row of medals onto the glass counter. With a cursory look at them she flounced out. Wath knew he was being watched. Behind the counter there was a net covered window at the back of the shelves through which the owner would be assessing him. Sure enough, a minute or two later an elderly man wearing a mask entered through the same door as the girl. He looked at the medals from a distance then held out a hand containing a white hospital mask.

'If you would be so kind.'

Wath put the mask on and immediately felt like a robber. Once the mask was in place the man approached the counter and examined the medals.

'Quite impressive, who's are they?'

'Mine.'

'No, I mean who were they awarded to'

'Me.'

Winfield raised his eyes from the counter looking the man up and down appraising him in minute detail. His clothes were tired and ill fitting. His fair hair was cropped in a military cut above a boyish face which looked as though he had still to start shaving. Despite his youthful appearance there were scars on his neck, on his right cheek now hidden by the mask and around his left eye. Nothing severely disfiguring just statements. The eyes dominated the face and Winfield found he could only hold them for a second or two. The intensity, the focus radiating from them was disconcerting. He was sure he had seen them before. He returned to business.

On the counter before him were an Oak Leaf and a Distinguished Conduct Medal, both medals awarded for bravery and gallantry in the field, but alongside them were a Military Medal and a Military Cross. One was for men in the ranks, the other for officers although this could include non-commissioned officers. It was a very unlikely combination. A glimmer of recognition surfaced.

'You've been here before. You sold me stolen goods. You were on the boats.' Dyson neither moved nor commented. Winfield shrugged, what was past was past, there was a row of medals in front of him and a decision to be made.

'Have you proof these are yours?'

Dyson took out three pieces of paper, old press cuttings and unfolded them at the side of the medals. In each there was a photograph of a soldier holding a medal with a brief summary underneath. Winfield picked them up and compared the photographs to the face in front of him. He put the papers down and looked at the stringy young man waiting patiently.

'Are you this Wath Dyson?' he said pointing at the papers.

'I am.'

'And you want to sell all of these?'

'I do.'

'I'll give you ten pounds for the lot.'

'No.'

Winfield was now certain it was the youth who came in from time to time several years ago brazenly touting stolen goods. Back then the youth always had a valuation in mind, usually fair, reflecting the status of the goods he was selling.

'How much?'

'Twelve gold sovereigns and four half crowns. I don't like paper money.'

'Eleven sovereigns but I want to keep the cuttings as well.'

'You asked how much, it's that or I'm going.'

That left no doubt, it was him. 'Alright but you sign to say there are authentic.'

'Agreed.'

Winfield took a piece of paper out from a drawer in the counter and wrote a declaration upon it with a new style fountain pen then passed it for Wath to inspect. He read it and passed it back.

'You spelt authentic wrong.'

Winfield snatched the paper, scanned it and looked at Wath in amazement. 'So, I have.'

He rewrote the note, Wath signed it and Winfield counted the money across along with a receipt. As Wath moved to the door Winfield scooped the medals into the drawer behind the counter and called 'Wait! Tell me the Military Cross and Military medal. What did you do to get them?'

Wath stared at him for a full ten seconds before answering 'Something I want to forget.' He turned, exited and closed the door.

Jumping off the train Wath strode across the platform and onto Station Road before Smalley finished his flag waving. Striding briskly over the canal bridge to the top of Station Road he turned left towards Manvers. He passed familiar land marks, nodding politely to the people he met. Re crossing the canal at Gore Hill Bridge, he went past Common Lane to the general store at the top of Winifred Street. Inside he asked for tobacco, potatoes, carrots, onion, swede, a tin of corned beef, Bovril, butter, half a pound of sugar and a bag of flour. A young girl he did not recognise served him placing it all inside a cardboard box. Armed with provisions he ambled down Common Lane and crossed the railway line back into Treacle Town and home.

Once inside he peeled potatoes, carrots, onion and swede and placed them in a pan with water. Stirring in a good spoonful of Bovril he carefully opened the corned beef. Whoever designed the tins wanted thrashing, they were lethal. Safely navigating the beef out of the tin, he deposited it in the pan and put the pan on the fire after poking it into life then covering the coals with a layer of slack to produce a long-lasting simmer.

He took all the peelings outside to the communal hen run and threw them for the chickens, they hurled themselves at the trimmings fighting and battling for the scraps. They were starving. He looked inside the hutch. There were twelve eggs. Twelve eggs from three hens meant they had not been tended in a while. He gathered eight eggs and took four of them inside before placing the other four outside Jimmy Cotton's door.

'Jimmy, you alright.' He called through the door.

'Aye' came a faint reply

'Eggs outside.'

'Ta.' Was the only response.

Wath then went to the Jenkinson's and hammered on the door. After thirty or forty seconds without a response he walked to the end of the yard and looked up at the signal box. Frank was looking down

24

at him through an open window. 'Couple o minutes, got to let the three o'clock through.'

He sat on the bottom step of the signal box stairs and rolled himself a cigarette. Smoking it he watched the signal in the distance. After a minute the horizontal arm on the top of the post fell until it was pointing at the floor. Thirty seconds later a mainline engine pulling a dozen carriages trundled past and the signal reverted back to horizontal. Frank descended the stairs.

'Ten minutes before Wath Main to Mexborough power station.'

Wath nodded knowingly and they both approached the door of the Jenkinson's.

'Got a mask?' asked Frank. Wath pulled the white hospital mask from his pocket. 'Put it on and don't touch anything.' Frank ordered. Wath watched as Frank pulled the sleeves of his jumper over his hands and opened the door.

'Ron, Ron, you there?' he called entering the house with Wath at his heels, 'Lilly, Lilly it's Frank, you ok?'

The house was eerily still, the very air moribund. Pots lay on the table, pans in the sink, a burnt-out fire in the hearth. Frank looked into the front room, shook his head and pointed up the stairs.

'Lilly, Ron it's me Frank I'm coming up, you ok?'

Wath trailed him up the stairs, there was a smell, a smell that he knew. He prepared himself for the inevitable. At the top Frank turned into the bedroom and stopped, his body rigid, his expression pained. Wath followed him through the door. Lilly was in bed her mouth agape, her face grey, Ron was on the floor, still in his pyjamas, as if collapsed trying to get to the door. Wath watched Frank shudder his face drained of colour, 'Got to check them.'

'They're dead Frank.'

'But… you don't know, we gotta… we gotta check.'

'Frank, I know, I seen enough dead.'

They walked back to the signal box and both sat deep in their own thoughts. Frank changed the signals for the Wath Main to Mexborough train then made a brew for them both.

'Who do we tell?' asked Wath.

'Police' said a chastened Frank, tears brimming in his eyes. 'They confirm Spanish Flu then sort everything out.'

'Is it still Goulding?'

'Aye.'

'I'll go tell him.'

'Don't go upsetting him, he don't like you as it is.'

'Aye.'

Wath walked back up Common Lane, the fifteen-foot red brick wall along the right-hand side hid the glassworks though he could see the smoke from the furnaces and smell Stanley's Soap and Oil factory behind it. On the left-hand side terraced houses lined the road. There were no gardens at the front just flag stones hiding coal cellars. He ignored Edna Street which led through the terrace onto Winifred Road which ran parallel with Common Lane.

At the top of the lane where it met Doncaster Road, he turned left passed the shop and at the next house knocked on the door. After a long few seconds, it was opened by a huge man only half dressed, his trousers held up by bracers over a vest. He was shoeless and obviously chewing on something difficult to digest. He looked down at Wath

'Heard you was back... come to give yourself up?'

Wath ignored him instead looking up and down Doncaster Road uncomfortable to be seen talking to a policeman.

'Well! What? Not got all day.'

'The Jenkinson's.'

'Yeah.'

'They're dead.'

'How?'

Wath shrugged 'Flu?' he turned to walk away.

'Oy.' Wath stopped 'Cause any trouble and I'll kick seven shades of shit out o you.'

The policeman was easily six foot tall, barrel chested, an ox of a man. His arms were thick and strong, each hand large enough to hold a baby in, his face marked by the times he had fought drunks, separated fighting miners and arrested hard men. Wath looked up at him.

'You'll try.' he said in a voice which was disturbingly quiet, ominously unconcerned and laced with menace.

After leaving Constable Goulding he didn't feel like going home so Wath walked to The Lord Nelson, one of two pubs in Nash Row as the gaggle of houses trapped between the railway lines and the canal was known. He pushed the door open and walked to the bar, a pretty barmaid smiled at him from behind it.

'Yes love, what can I get you?'

'Pint please,'

He watched her pull the long-handled pump and fill the glass up to the brim.

'That'll be four pence, can I get you anything else?' she said with her hands on her hips, one leg bent, her torso leant forward seductively, her blouse pulled tight across her chest and tucked neatly into a skirt belted on her slim waist. Jet-black hair was tied back in a bun with whisps falling temptingly across her face as large brown eyes smiled at him.

'Fine thanks.'

He took his pint and parked himself on the bench seat under the window. There were three elderly men sat at a table all drinking pints and surveying him surreptitiously, an unopened box of dominoes in front of them. After a few minutes when he was a third of the way down his pint one of the men bent towards him.

'Do you play lad, fancy a game?'

He shrugged, why not.

Two pints later, with Wath a full shilling and nine pence down, a fourth man entered, obviously the last member of the team. Wath

27

held his hands up 'Too good for me boys.' And moved over to let the new man in. He finished his beer and stood up to go.

'Tha can come again, anytime.' Said the man who had asked him to play, a gleeful smile on his lips. Wath grinned, they had spotted a patsy and were keen to empty his pockets.

'Aye, maybe.' He left and walked home. The corned beef hash was cooked to a treat with the smell greeting him as he entered the yard. He didn't bother with a plate, eating straight out of the pan. Half way down his appetite was satisfied and he poured the rest into a bowl. Taking it outside he placed it on Jimmy's door step and banged on the door. The eggs he had placed there earlier were gone.

'Some hash here Jimmy' he called 'don't let it go cold.'

Not bothering to wait for a reply he went back into the kitchen, mended the fire and curled into his chair done for the night.

Chapter Four

Wednesday 18/2/1920

He slept soundly and woke when the main line train from Barnsley trundled past the front room. Six o'clock. With nowhere to go and no rush to get there he made the fire back up and moulded a rough dough from his flour with butter, sugar and eggs. On the top shelf over the cellar there was a jar of currants so he threw a handful in and made half a dozen patties. Wiping a frying pan clean he placed it on the fire and dry grilled the patties two at a time. He ate three, washing them down with a cup of tea, then took the remainder down the yard placing them on the step and collecting the empty bowl from last night.

'Breakfast, you idle bugger.' He shouted and went back to wash the pots.

Checking the cellar, he realised he needed coal so he hunted around and found an old sack. He moved out of the yard following the rails past Wath Junction until he came to the colliery curve where the Great Central Line passed though the Manvers colliery crossing the Midland Line before merging with the Swinton and Knottingley section of the Midlands and North Eastern Line. He bent down and started picking up the coal spilled on the tracks where the wagons from Wath Main, Elsecar and Darfield Collieries negotiated the points and the bend at the same time. In less than a minute his sack was full and he headed back.

On his return he looked in on the hens. There were only two, a freshly pecked carcass evidence of what had happened. There was only one new egg so he took it with the others. Sitting on the back step he rolled a cigarette and enjoyed the taste. The seven o'clock

Doncaster to Barnsley via Wath clattered past on the Great Central line.

Two doors down he heard a plate rattle and saw Jimmy putting it back on the step. He was pale and drawn, feeble looking, a sheen of sweat on his brow. He looked across to Wath.

'Thanks lad.' Wath nodded and returned to his smoke.

He decided to put the day to use. Over the next few hours, he walked the length and breadth of the Town. He avoided Whitworths Brewery where Lucy's father worked but called in at Stanley's Soap and Oil factory, Waterstones glass works, McIndoe's metal refinishers, Elgin's scrap yard, Wath Main, the Coke Ovens and finally Manvers Main. Everywhere was the same, there were no jobs. Hundreds of thousands killed or maimed in the war many more hundreds of thousands dying of Spanish Flu and still jobs were scarce.

As the day ended, frustrated but unsurprised, Wath called in The Lord Nelson again. The young barmaid smiled even wider and the team of four were concentrating on their game. Wath took his pint and sat alongside them watching them play. After a few games it became clear they were all experts, counting the dominoes, anticipating who had what and drawing them out. He realised he had been an easy mark and it would be a long time before he could compete with this lot.

Two very young men came in and stood at the bar, they were too young to drink but the girl served them none the less. One of them kept looking at Wath without wanting to be seen doing so. The youth ordered another pint and walked over standing directly in front of Wath, pint in hand.

'You Wath Dyson?'

Wath looked him up and down sixteen maybe seventeen, skinny, pock marked.

'Aye.'

'This is for you then.' The youth said holding out the pint. Wath looked at him quizzically. 'From me Dad... he said if I ever met you in a pub, I was to buy you a pint from him.'

Wath stretched out his arm and took the pint.

'Who's your dad?'

'Harold, Harold Braithwaite.'

Wath nodded slowly, remembering a tall thin man with an infectious smile and quick wit. A man he spent three days and two nights with, trapped in a bomb crater in no man's land. They sat powerless as bombs and bullets flew all around them unable to move as Harold's gut shot brother was lying in agony at the side of the crater. When the fighting quietened, they took it in turns to carry him out.

He banished the memories.

He was not going back.

'Aye. A good man. Tell him thanks.'

'He says you were best man he ever met, best man to have at your side.'

Wath smiled appreciatively 'That's nice but he's wrong, your Uncle Albert were better.'

The youth looked at him with fresh eyes, surprised that the man sitting in front of him could remember someone who died in the trenches over three years ago. He nodded and turned back to his mate at the bar, both chatting with the girl before leaving with a small wave. Wath drank the pint and as he placed the empty glass on the table the girl behind the bar shouted. 'Another?'

He nodded and she pulled the pint then carried it over to the table. As she returned to the bar the closest member of the domino team leant across to him.

'You'll be alright there, lad. She'll keep thi warm on a night.'

Wath smiled and looked across at the girl. There were worse things to think about.

Chapter Five

Thursday 19/2/1920

The next morning, he sat on his step again wondering what the day would bring. There was a disturbance at the end of the yard. It was the Undertakers carrying body bags from the end house. He watched the hearse leaving the Jenkinson's. That was one job he definitely did not want. The pandemic had caused a surge in burials but the men who collected the bodies were vulnerable to the disease and suffering more than most. No, he could leave that one alone.

He considered walking the canal to see if any of the boats were still working but decided against it. He had moved on from that life years ago. The year when his Mam's fella died. He never called him dad just Locke. He remembered the night, people everywhere, all looking into the canal, the Police using a boat hook to grab the floating bundle of rags that was Locke.

Drunk, again, he had stopped by some bushes to relieve himself, something had disturbed him and as he turned, he slipped and fell into the canal. His flies were still open when they fished him out. After Locke's death the barge owner refused to rent him and his Mam the boat. "Not to a woman and that young shite house." No, his boating days were over.

The problem was that after yesterday's walk it didn't leave much else and Goulding was going to blame him for anything that went wrong or missing. But at least he had reserves to keep him going before it came to exploiting the "sticky opportunities" as his Mam used to call them.

Returning inside, as the seven thirty London to Leeds toiled past on the North Eastern Line, he was just brewing tea when the door opened and a man in a mask entered without knocking. Despite the mask and the four years since he had last seen him Wath knew instantly who the man was, Suggett the landlord's rent collector.

'Who're you?' the rent collector asked without ceremony.

'Take a guess.'

'Mr Smart Alec.' Suggett countered sarcastically.

'That'll do. But you know who I am.'

'You need to leave cos I'm here to board the house up.'

'I'm staying.'

Suggett looked at him with sheer disgust.

'Ok, Mr Smart Alec there's three month's rent owing on this house. you can start by paying that and then you'd better be ready cos it's going to be demolished soon and I'm not bothered whether you're inside or out when we do.'

Wath nodded but said nothing. The man was stood inside the door with all the confidence of the largest bully in the school yard. He was leant forward with his hands on his hips thrusting the chin of his huge head out with a sneer riding his lips. His jacket had leather patches at the elbows and down the thighs his blue trousers were a faded grey through use. The boots showing under them were so worn and scuffed the metal toecaps showed through the leather. A pocket watch tucked into one waist coat pocket with a chain across to the other side was the only decoration and even here the end clasp of the chain was bent and broken, half missing. He turned, looking hard at Wath, a curious expression across his face.

'What happened to the Jenkinson's?'

'Flu.'

'They gone?'

'Aye.'

'Ok, you can stay. We'll board them up instead. I'll be back in half an hour when we've done. Have the money ready.'

Wath didn't move, he stayed sat in the armchair blowing on the hot tea in his mug. As the man reached the door he called. 'Before you go, leave me Mam's pocket watch on the table.'

'What?'

'You heard. Leave the watch on the table.'

Suggett stopped at the door, glaring at Wath, his left hand making an involuntary twitch towards the watch.

'You'd better be careful. Making accusations like that.'

Wath shrugged. 'We both know it's got engraving on the inside and we both know what it says.'

'You don't know that.' There was sheer hatred in his eyes.

'Yes, I do. It was me that broke that clasp. So, put it on the table before I take it off you.'

'Oh yeah!'

'Oh yeah' echoed Wath calmly nodding 'and this is your last chance. If I get out of this chair you won't get out of the yard.'

Wath took a drink of his tea staring at the rent collector over the mug. His eyes were alive, the light from them piercing Suggett, challenging him, daring him to carry on. Suggett stood transfixed the strut and sneer slowly replaced with hesitation, indecision.

Wath had seen it before, all bullies were cowards at heart and this one was no different. They both knew the inscription on the watch. Suggett was working out what would happen if he and the occupant of this almost derelict house came tumbling into the yard with Wath calling him a thief and demanding proof in front of witnesses. They both knew what the repercussions of that would be. His job lost, his chance to brag and strut gone. Wath watched the bully wilt, it showed in his eyes first, then his mouth and finally in his stance.

Suggett slowly pulled the watch from his waistcoat pocket and placed it on the table.

Wath continued to drink his tea 'and you can cancel the owed rent, I presume you found money in me mother's clothes so forget coming back for more, you'll not be getting one penny o rent from me. You can tell your Bosses why... if you want.'

Suggett turned but stopped at the door. 'You just made yourself an enemy.'

'Join the queue.' Wath answered brightly.

34

Determined not to waste the day Wath walked into Town itself. After a brief stroll up and down the High Street he went into the library. It was only two rooms separated by a corridor with the walls of both covered in shelves lined with books. There was a table in each with chairs around them and in the larger of the two rooms another table where an elderly lady sat organising a raft of books. He looked around bemused not sure whether to open the door or not. The elderly woman saw him through the glass and opened the door making his decision for him.

'Can I help?' she enquired as they performed an intricate dance to keep their distance from one another rather than put their masks on.

'I'd like to join and borrow a book.'

'Do you live in Wath?' he nodded 'Ok I'll take your details and that will be fine.'

As they filled in the form her friendly attitude cooled when he gave his address as Treacle Town and positively froze when he gave his name. She was trapped by her earlier warmth and forced to show him how the system worked and give him his Library ticket. As a new lender he was only allowed one book at a time so Wath retreated into the other room, put his back to the door and pulled several books off the shelves trying to decide which one to take.

He was still sat mulling over the books when a woman and her daughter entered the far room. He was concentrating so hard he did not notice her open the door and walk around the table looking at the books on the shelves. She pulled a book down and turned towards the table, as she did, he looked up and stopped breathing, stunned.

It was Lucy.

She had a cloche hat over a fashionable bun style cut to her hair and wore a drop waist dress with a long cardigan over the top, all covered by an expensive looking coat. He couldn't see them but he guessed her shoes were sensible yet stylish. Her face was scrubbed

35

and pink as though with a pale blusher, but this was natural. Not a hint of mascara around her eyes just a demur red lipstick highlighting her mouth. Nothing coarse or overbearing, everything was delicate and understated but perfect.

As she turned a trace of perfume drifted across the table, it was subtle holding the tiniest hint of lemon making it fresh. Her features were still beautifully proportioned, her oval face enhanced by a smooth jaw line, large wide eyes framing a small straight nose above full lips and a small jutting chin. There were a few tiny lines that he did not remember but they enhanced her looks rather than detracted. Her skin shone with a healthy well-fed glow. She was a young woman at her finest.

He felt shabby alongside her. He had never considered the need to dress well, he could never afford it, but the old jacket, crumpled shirt and tired trousers above army boots were stale. Stale looking and stale smelling. He curled his hands turning his fingers into the palms so she would not see the filth under his nails. Then he remembered he had not had a proper wash since he returned, a quick rinse in cold water at the sink was all. He stank and felt and looked like a tramp. He finally sucked in air and begged for the chair to swallow him as he shrank into it.

Lucy locked eyes with the man sat at the table, recognition flowing like electricity whizzed between them, sparking, a small gasp involuntarily escaping from her mouth. Then a grim cloud fell over her, an icy blast flowing through her body. Here was the man she had loved without boundaries, the one man who could do no wrong, but that was before he left, before he went to war.

He had changed but she couldn't say how. The same boyish veneer perhaps with a fiercer expression on what had always been a serious face, the same startling blue eyes that still held yours in a vice like grip. There were scars on the face which hadn't been there before and she realised it was these that made the expression harder.

36

They didn't seriously spoil or take away his good looks they just made him seem world weary as though he had seen everything.

The hair, the clothes, they all looked the same, in fact she could swear the clothes were the same as the ones he left in. They certainly smelled old, a four-year-old musk that hadn't matured well. He was slightly thinner than she recalled and certainly grimier, he was trying to hide his hands but they were filthy. Broken finger nails stained black, each holding enough dirt to plant seeds in.

Even when they were at their lowest, surviving on whatever could be stolen, living from day to day, she had not seen him this grubby. She could see from the way he was reacting, trying to disappear, that he was uncomfortable and that he was as surprised as she was at meeting.

She recovered first and nodded. 'Wath.'

'Lucy.' It was said with a sigh underpinned with reverence.

'Didn't know you were back.' Her tone was hard, spiky.

'Couple o days.'

She looked down at the books in front of him. 'Didn't know you could read.'

'Army has it's uses.'

He was answering quickly, factually, hiding behind his words. She could see he was thinking how to get out of this, how to avoid her questions.

'Teach you to write as well?' He nodded. 'So why didn't you?' Her tone moved from spiky it was now confrontational, even nasty.

'Couldn't, when I could, wouldn't let me.'

'Who? Who wouldn't let you? Nobody ever stopped you doing anything before!' she spat.

Here we go the same old Wath - it was somebody else's fault, as if that made it right? He wasn't getting away with it this time. No, he may have done in the past but not now, not after four years without contact. Leaving her with his mother, pregnant and with a young child to bring up in that hell hole. She seethed, four years of pent-up frustration boiling inside.

37

She held her breath, charting a way forward, wanting to pick her words, to make them hurt. An awkward silence evolved where neither knew what to say. A young girl walked in. Her entrance cutting through the atmosphere like the iron prow of a ship crashing waves through pack ice. 'Mummy, mummy she says I can have two books now!'

She had an imitation sailor style dress on with a warm woollen coat over it and a beret on her head. Her hair was a waterfall of golden ringlets cascading over her shoulders and down her back. The ice blue eyes looked huge in the small dimpled face.

Lucy cuddled the girl into her dress. She watched Wath stare, his mouth open, his expression changing from aggrieved contrition to one of awe. Lucy gathered the girl in, a cattiness bordering on sheer malice drove her next words 'Alice, say hello, this is your father.'

The girl turned and looked at him, her eyes wide with an expectant glint but as she examined him a puzzled frown arced across her brow.

'Why are you crying?' the young girl asked.

Lucy savoured his reaction, relished his discomfort. Wath was choked, his throat appeared paralysed and large individual tears were crawling down his cheeks. 'I don't... I don't know.' was the best he could manage after a deep breath.

'Go chose your books please. I'll be out in a minute' ordered Lucy gently pushing the young girl into the other room and closing the door behind her. Turning back to Wath, who was sat crumpled with tears snaking down his cheeks, she could barely disguise a victorious smirk as she asked 'You alright?' noting with anger the very faintest tinge of compassion in her voice.

'I... yeah. She's... so beautiful.'

Lucy nodded. 'I think so too.' She sat down, watching him intently.

'Why Lucy? Why?' he asked.

He... he... was asking why, as if she was the one who had to explain, as if she was to blame, as if it was her fault. She glared at

38

the tear-stained face noticing the way the scars now stood out as his complexion reacted to the tears. She recalled the scars across his back, the marks from birch lashes in his youth. Eighteen in total, she had counted them one by one, run her fingers down them. Well, if she could put enough venom in her voice to make it slash and slice there would be more, many more. She tore into him her tone spiteful, mean, as vicious as she could make it.

'Because I was fed up of waiting, fed up of your fucking silence, fed up of being ignored, left ignorant of what you were doing. For Christs sake Wath, the war ended over two years ago and you've only just got back. Not a word, not one word since you left. Even when Arthur was born, even when he died. Not a word, not one fucking word!'

She slammed her book onto the table and folded her arms, ramming her back into the chair, leering at him as he fixed his stare onto the table top.

A silence grew which seemed to stretch the no man's land between them while at the same time filling it with an invisible fog. A thick clawing fog that weighed you down, a poisonous uncrossable fog.

Tears were still dripping down his cheeks but Wath appeared oblivious to them. She watched, drinking in every tear, enjoying every one, tasting it, revelling in each, each a drop of satisfaction.

Eventually he looked up, looking her in the eye.

'Sorry.'

Lucy's mouth fell open. 'I don't believe this' she said after a few beats of her heart 'is that really you? Crying. Saying sorry. What the fuck did they do to you over there. It's nice but it's not you.' This was not the man she was used to. This was not the way she expected their first meeting to go. When he first went to war, she had prepared herself for never seeing him again, but since then, if he came back, she had planned screaming and ranting, slapping and hurting, kicking and gouging, not listening to apologies.

She gathered herself for another assault. 'Do you want to know what he looked like, what he sounded like, your son, the son you never saw – do you want to know!'

'Yes please.'

'Yes please, yes fucking please! Damn you Wath. Ask your bitch of a mother.'

'She's dead.'

She hesitated for the briefest of seconds. 'Flu?'

He nodded.

'Can't say the world is missing much.' She said dismissively before standing up. 'Got to go.'

'Can I see Alice again… please.'

He hadn't made a comment about her or where she was living, what she was doing, about them, about the past, what he'd done, where he'd been, just sorry can he see Alice again. Oh, and please, don't forget the please.

'I'll have to think. I'll have to ask Henry.' He didn't react to that either, it was as if something was missing, there was nothing inside him, he was empty, this wasn't the man she remembered. The gorgeous cocky unpredictable loving rascal. The man everyone hated but who had enough love hidden inside to balance the scales. The man who could carry the bile of the world single handed and not bend. The man who would face the devil and smile. No this wasn't even a shadow of the man she remembered, 'I'll let you know.'

He simply nodded, the tears still running down his face. She turned, collected her daughter and after a long look back, left him crying at the table.

Forgetting to take a book and almost staggering out of the library Wath walked blindly past the green grocers, the banks and the Saracens Head finding himself outside the church. The church had been started in the twelve century and added to every century since. All the additions were made in the same Yorkshire sandstone and had been stained black by coal smoke over the years making the building appear cheerless and grim. The huge porch with its stone seats was open and Wath stared. He started towards the entrance then stopped.

God could not help him.

Slowly he changed direction and moved around the side of the bell tower. The disused prison showed over the wall and as he passed the tower a large dark grave dominated the pathway ahead. Abel Dyson. He gazed at the huge head stone and the coping stone of the false tomb covering the grave. The cost of the grave must have been enormous. The stone work was immaculate and the position shouted respect. But no more. A day-old child had stopped all that.

He sighed and walked past. He jumped over the wall to the lane by the old prison and followed it down to the canal.

At the brewery bridge he sat on a low wall and watched the water, his thoughts wandering. This was the place where Locke had died all them years ago, the place where him and his Mam finally left the boats.

He picked up a stone and threw it into the canal. It made a blop sound and disappeared below the surface. He watched the ripples spread and dissipate. Temporary patterns creating a small insignificant life soon gone. Like his life on the boats.

The life he lived before the war was no way to continue, scraping a living, going hungry, despised. Lucy had left him and she looked wonderful. That was what he needed – money and status - a standing in life. Like Henry had, like Abel presumably had before he died. He reflected upon the last few days since his return and realised that just burning his uniform and selling his medals were not enough, he needed to change.

Too quickly he defaulted to violence. His automatic reaction was to challenge, to attack. But in the library, he had seen what he wanted and collapsed. Unable to attack his usually impenetrable façade proved completely useless. He wanted respect but most of all he needed Lucy back in his life. He needed to hear Alice laugh and sing and dance. Right now, his life was empty, a waste of space.

He dug into his pocket and pulled out a coin, a sixpence. He blew a kiss on it and threw it into the canal for luck. He would change, he would make something of himself and he would start now.

But how?

Depression pressed on him from all sides. It was all well and good wanting, dreaming, but he could not see how to achieve his ambitions. The world around him was set, everyone knew their place in life. No one broke the mould and his place had been set on day one. On Abel's gravestone.

From the raised vantage point of the signal box Frank watched Wath cross the railway line and walk back into Treacle Town. There was something about his walk that was concerning. He seemed distant, unaware of his surroundings, an air of dejection following him like the wake behind a ship or the tremor of a train on the track after it had passed.

The young lad who kept him company before the war had an indomitable spirit, no matter what the world threw at him. When assailed he regrouped inside his ring of steel - the railways lines which cut off but protected the seven houses. Perhaps, thought Frank, that was what he was doing now. He certainly looked as if he was. In his youth his cocksure attitude and permanently serious expression was a defence mechanism which those who knew him ignored and waited for the quick laugh and self-deprecating humour, but now his shoulders were slumped, his walk tired and slow as if dragging a dead weight.

Frank thought about shouting him, calling him up for a mug of tea but decided against it. Wath was the deepest person he knew. If he didn't want to talk about something then he didn't. It was that simple. There was nothing that could make him talk. You waited and when he was ready – if he ever became ready - he talked.

42

It was ten years since him and his Mam had walked into the yard and taken the end terrace. His Mam's fella, Locke, had died and they had been thrown off the boat by the owner. Frank recalled Locke's death, a drunken drowning. From what he gleaned it was not unusual for him to be drunk but he must have been blinding that night because boatmen were notoriously careful around their boats. Few of them could swim so the water was their worst nightmare. Frank heard later that Wath's Mam must have seen it happen but waited half an hour before she went to the nearest house and raised the alarm. It would not surprise him if this was true. She had a streak in her, vicious, cruel, vengeful.

When they arrived in Treacle Town Wath was only twelve years old but looked younger. A tiny frame, an angelic face and an innocent air hid a steely determination, an insatiable curiosity and a capacity for trouble which a hardened criminal would have difficulty matching. Even at that tender age he was a veteran of the Judicial system and had suffered the birch several times. Three lashes for shop lifting, another six for pick pocketing and nine for larceny. His mother was on probation with an instruction to control him while Locke had once been fined ten shillings for failing in his duty to raise the child properly.

On his first day in the yard a curious Wath had climbed the steps of the signal box and looked in, eager to understand his new surroundings. Frank had been bored so he waved the youngster in and chatted to him. He was skin and bones with eyes sunk into his cheeks, blue piercing eyes that flittered around the room constantly landing on Franks sandwiches. He remembered asking him how long it had been since he'd eaten. Yesterday, a boiled egg for breakfast was the reply. The offer to share his sandwiches brought about the first grin Frank saw on his face. The lad devoured the sandwich and the apple Frank gave him, even the core, pips and all. After that day he always packed an extra sandwich and Wath became a regular visitor regardless of what shift Frank was on.

43

But Frank was aware of the reputation the two newcomers brought with them so he gave the youngster a warning 'you rob or burgle around here and we fall out for good.' and in a seemingly guileless reply the twelve-year-old Wath looked him in the eye and said, 'you don't shit on your own doorstep Mister.' And he never had. Not once had the lad done anything wrong inside Treacle Town.

Frank had watched him grow, heard his voice break and witness him develop into a young man with eyes that young girls simply fell into. One look and they were captivated but Wath was oblivious to it all, too busy surviving - until he met Lucy. Then he was as trapped as she was. The rest of the world disappeared and they only saw each other. When the inevitable happened and she fell pregnant with Alice, she moved in with him and his Mam. They were both still kids, only sixteen when Alice was born, but very happy kids.

Then at the beginning of 1916, to avoid a court appearance which promised prison, Wath volunteered and went to the war in France leaving Lucy behind, three months pregnant and Alice a toddler. Rumours kept surfacing from the injured and maimed who returned about how bravely Wath fought but for Lucy the war was a battle fought in the trenches of Treacle Town. A losing battle. Constantly berated by Wath's Mam she could do no right.

Wath had always been able to control his mother, keep her at bay, but without him there she poured venom onto Lucy. There was no let up, even when she gave birth to a son, Arthur, then Arthur contacted whooping cough and died before his second birthday and that was when Lucy cracked. She was an attractive woman and Henry Mallinder, a rich middle-aged man chased her every day. One day she left Treacle Town without a word, moving in with Henry and moving up in life. Moving away from squalor into a comfortable lifestyle with everything provided.

And all the time nothing was heard from Wath.

Now the lad was back and old wounds were being reopened. There was no doubt he had always been a rascal, his upbringing guaranteed that, but their contact had been confined to the stranded island of Treacle Town and to Frank he was the son he never had.

As his thoughts settled there were footsteps on the stairs, Wath opened the door and walked in, sitting on the window sill at the far end of the box. Frank openly assessed him waiting for the right moment to talk. After a few minutes Wath sighed, that was all the signal Frank needed.

'You alright lad? You look a bit fed up if you ask me.'

'Aye.'

'You want to talk about it? You know … over there … get it out of your system?'

'Made a promise to myself, never going back there, not talking about it, ever, never gunna be that person again.'

He was rolling a cigarette, a simple enough procedure that he had done a thousand times without looking but this time he was doing it with determination and concentration enough to complete the Times crossword.

'I've just seen Lucy and Alice.'

Frank didn't say a word just watched, watched Wath's brow furrow further, the words were casually uttered but the undertone was full of passion and meaning. Awe? Astonishment? Wonder?

'Tell me about Henry Mallinder.' Wath at his best: same subject different angle.

'What do you want to know? He's approaching forty that's both his belly in inches and his age in years. Still got a full head of hair though. That the kind of stuff you want?'

'What's he do?' This was the question he really wanted to ask. Where he was really heading towards and if Frank was reading it right, that the lad still harboured feelings for Lucy, then this was going to hurt.

'Started a concrete business. It's done really well. You know through the bends past Manvers on the way to Mexborough he's got a plant there. He borrowed some money from Percy Shaw and built a factory. Was really clever, started by renting a sand pit and then

45

began taking the ash from the glass works and brewery. Took it away at no charge and used it to bulk out his cement, was able to be the cheapest around. Then he started making concrete pipes, you know for drainage and the like. Got a contract with both pits and the coke ovens then the water works and the Council. They reckon he's making a fortune. There's even rumours of concrete houses being built in West Melton.'

'So where do they live?'

Everything he was saying was pushing Lucy and Alice further away from the life Wath could offer them but Frank couldn't hide anything. The lad would find out anyway and he had an aptitude for absorbing blunt truisms that was essential in a life as hard as his.

'Fitzwilliam Street, got a stone detached house with gardens on the right-hand side going up. Opposite the pheasantry.'

Frank watched Wath retreat into himself. The eyes dimmed over as he sank into his thoughts. The as yet unexplained scars hardened the still boyish expression and placed a layer of disquiet across his features. It might just be his imagination but now when Wath squinted or narrowed his eyes there was a sinister suggestion, a glimmer of the menace lurking underneath. The illusion of innocence had been removed.

'You're not thinking of doing anything daft are you lad?'

'Nah, never done anything daft in my entire life. Not gunna start now.'

Chapter Six

Friday 13/3/1920

On the Friday morning Wath left three hard boiled eggs on Jimmy's door step and placing the rest in his pocket set off towards Mexborough. His plan was to walk through the town visiting all the places where employment could be found. There had to be a job out there somewhere.

He took the road through Manvers and after the bends stood for a long time looking through the fence at the concrete works. Twentieth Century Concrete, a sign above the gate proudly announced. There was a large warehouse with a several storage bays at the side and a long open sided unit where all kinds of things made in concrete were left to dry.

The whole scene looked well organised and efficient with a relaxed casual atmosphere. Storage bays were covered with canvas tarpaulins, bricks stacked in neat piles, tools leant in haphazard fashion against the rear wall. There was enough room under the canopied roof to work but the open sides meant the men were outside most of the time and the cement dust they inevitably created blew harmlessly across the yard.

As he watched a cart pulled in and deposited sand into one of the bays, then a flat-bed lorry stopped outside the warehouse and two men, one of them definitely unsuited to manual labour, came out to unload the bags of cement from the back of the lorry carrying them into the warehouse. The overweight man noticed him watching and walked over, his balding forehead covered in sweat even though he had only just started unloading the wagon.

'You after a job?'

'Why?'

'Got a vacancy for a labourer if you want. But you have to start now. Idle bastard ant turned up again. Got another delivery on the way. Flat rate a shilling an hour.'

'Nah thanks.'

Wath turned and walked away the fat man's curses echoing as he walked.

Mexborough was as barren as Wath upon Dearne. The water works, glass works, gas works, railway sheds, Queens Foundry, Don Valley Pottery, Don Chemicals and the two Iron and Steel works all closed their gates to new employees. He argued with one man at the railway sheds who demanded he have a union card before he asked for a job.

'How do I get a card?'

'Get a job' was the answer. Not only were the owners and bosses picking and choosing their employees but now their workers were deciding who got jobs. He kicked a stone at the futility of it all. Giving up he returned home via Swinton taking the canal path for the last leg of the journey. The sun glinted on the water and for a time he lost himself in memories.

It was mid-afternoon as he crossed the railway lines back into Treacle Town. Frank was sat on the bottom step to the signal box.

'Thought I'd missed you' he said in greeting. 'been waiting nearly an hour.'

Wath looked at him bemused. Frank was on the early shift this week and should have been gone two hours ago never mind one.

'Do you want a job?' Frank asked.

'That's second time that's been said to me today' Wath smiled 'go on then what's the job?'

'Carting. Joe Whiteley's delivery lad got a job down pit and left, so he's looking for someone to look after a cart doing deliveries. Got to know horses. I told him you looked after horses on the barges and needed a job. I'll be honest, he weren't too keen at first but I vouched for you and he said he'd give you a go. Fancy it?'

48

'Aye, when and where and how much?'

'It's a shilling an hour and a five-bob bonus if you get all your deliveries done in the week. I'll take you up to meet him and you can arrange all that with him. He's got a stable at the back of Orchard Place in Townend. Come on we'll still catch him, if we're quick.'

Two hours later Wath pushed the door to the Lord Nelson open and nodded at Betty as she asked 'Usual?' Taking his pint to the bench seat alongside the domino table he watched for a while. When there was a break in the play as they reshuffled Wath asked 'What's a miner earn these days, Bill?'

'Bout ninety shillings a week. Why?'

'Just got me a job carting paying half that and was curious.'

'Don't bet on them getting that much longer lad, you might be out earning them soon.'

'Why?'

'There's a hard time coming. Governments giving the mines back to the Owners and they will cut wages for sure.'

One of the other players leant across. 'And you'll not cripple your lungs or break your back or get buried carting lad. Well done. Did you say you was buying us all a pint to celebrate?'

Wath laughed out loud. 'You've got a bloody cheek. I've got to work an extra week to make up for what you've taken off playing that bloody game!'

The four men chuckled then smiled knowingly as Betty came across with another pint for Wath, 'You'll be up for buying me a Mackeson later though.' she stated, her blouse top yawning as she leant across his table.

Half an hour later, while Betty was changing barrels down the cellar, Wath left and went to Lockwood's chippy. Buying fish and chips twice with a portion of batter bits he walked back to Treacle Town. Leaving one portion on Jimmy's step he threw the batter bits in for the chickens before poking the fire and putting a pan of water on to make tea. Suitably prepared he started on his fish and chips before curling up in his chair.

Chapter Seven

Saturday 21/2/1920

The following day Wath rolled up a towel and walked to the public indoor pool. The swimming baths had been built before the war and were a huge success. But Wath had never learned to swim so the attraction was much less, however today he was not swimming. Paying the twopence entrance fee, he bought a penny tablet of soap and went into the changing rooms. Stripping he went into the showers and stood under the warm water for a full ten minutes savouring the heat and gentle massage. Lathering up his soap he started on his hair and worked down his body scrubbing furiously.

The water at his feet turned black as dust and grime fell from him. After five minutes the water ran clear again so Wath gave himself the luxury of another five minutes under the shower then towelled dry. He felt fresh and clean before putting on his old clothes which held a peculiar odour and now felt hard and crusty. Ignoring this he rolled up his towel and started back into the town centre.

Refreshed and about to be employed the scene looked completely different to the one he had survey two days ago. His new found optimism led him to the library where this time he selected a book and accomplished the process of having it stamped and loaned to him. Robinson Crusoe by Daniel Defoe. It was time to have a bit of exotic escapism in his life.

As he shuffled through the door, he saw Lucy stood chatting to another woman outside Wards Fruit and Veg shop. There was no sign of Alice but by her side was a well-dressed large man. His clothes were tailor made and the expensive shoes underneath his crisply creased trousers were polished to a shine. A big man he filled his suit in all directions, Frank was right, the waist line showed a healthy appetite and a lack of manual labour. Wath realised that he closely resembled the man at the concrete works who had offered him a job.

Unsure what to do and wanting to avoid a confrontation Wath looked to cross the road, as he did Lucy turned and saw him. Unable to avoid her stare he nodded, then started to cross over. Lucy nodded back and the man at her side looked at him. A full head of dark black hair topped a round face with the start of a double chin. He had a rounded nose and his eyes were brown and curious. There was a confident calm air about him as he spoke to Lucy. When Lucy replied he looked harder at Wath, his air of calm removed and a look of sheer antipathy crossed his face.

Wath ignored him and continued across the road passing around the Red Lion towards the blacksmiths and away from Lucy. He turned left up Sandygate, he was going the wrong way but taking the long route back down Burman Road was better than walking past Lucy in four-year-old clothes and scruffy army boots.

Back home he spent an idle afternoon reading his book comfortable in the knowledge that he had a job and would be starting work the day after tomorrow. He had a large pan of mutton stew on the coals and when it came to sharing it with Jimmy, he was surprised to see that he was on his feet. Still cautiously placing the bowl on the step, he watched as Jimmy collected it with thanks.

He was a shadow of the man he remembered. His shirt was hanging off him, his cheek bones sticking out of his face, the skin under his eyes purple. A grey pallor stained his skin while a sheen of sweat washed it. Jimmy had been a barrel-chested man heavily muscled due to his job as a collier which entailed shovelling eight yards of coal a shift. Then he was trapped by a rock fall which crushed his left arm and ankle. The ankle set at an awkward angle which gave him a rolling gait while the arm had to be amputated. He now worked as day time gate keeper to the coke ovens and the lack of activity had initially brought a weight increase but this was all now gone.

'How're you feeling?' Wath queried.

'Getting there, it's a nasty bugger this one.' He pointed to the fresh boards on the Jenkinson's. 'What happened?'

'Flu.' Wath replied without embellishment.

'Shit. You be careful, hear me'

'Will do, get that inside yer, see yer later. Oh! have yer got any hen feed?'

'Aye. I'll leave it out.'

Wath nodded and returned to his book.

Later as the light dimmed and he found reading becoming a strain he walked up to the Nelson seeking company. The domino team were a man short but one of the young lads made up the numbers. Wath sat down and Harold Braithwaite's lad joined him.

'I told me dad I'd bought you that pint and he gave me a shilling so there's another there if you want it.'

'Nah, you and yer mate have one on yer dad, bet that don't happen too often.'

'No, it don't. You obviously know him.'

Wath smiled and changed the subject as the other youth joined them, the domino team now up to full muster.

'This is Jack and I'm Walt.' Wath nodded and signalled Betty for another beer. The door opened and two large men walked in. They made for the bar and looked around. Seeing Wath one of them walked back out of the pub while the other ordered four pints of bitter. The second man returned with two more large men followed by Henry Mallinder. The four men spread themselves across the back wall covering the area between the bar and the door.

Henry stood in front of them glaring at Wath.

The click and clack of dominoes stopped and the two young lads shuffled to the side.

It was the closest Wath had been to him and he was surprised. The man was powerfully built but gone to seed. Frank was close

53

with the forty-inch waist line which was well hidden under expensively-tailored pants. Everything about him was rounded and comfortable. Apart from the scowl on his face he looked like a man enjoying life. The trouble with that was men like him did not like their happy existence disturbing.

'I've come to tell you to stay away from Lucy.' Mallinder said without preamble.

Wath made no comment taking a sip of his beer.

'Did you hear me; you stay away from her.'

'What does Lucy say?' Wath asked in a calm gentle tone.

'Got nothing to do with Lucy. I'm telling you to stay away.'

Wath placed his pint on the table looking Mallinder straight in the face.

'I think I'll let Lucy be the judge o that.'

Mallinder looked fit to explode. 'You'll stay away.'

'Or what?'

'Or you'll be getting more scars on that pretty face o yours.'

'If that's the best you can do Mallinder, piss off.'

Mallinder fumed, he bossed men, he sacked them, they did what he said, when he said, how he said. No one told him to piss off. He turned to the four men. 'Sort him.' Then marched out of the door, an automobile could be heard starting and pulling away as the four men finished their pints all staring at Wath.

The largest put his empty pint pot down, took a step forward and pointed at Wath.

'Sorry but it's time laddie.'

Wath nodded. 'Mind if I finish my pint and we do it outside. Don't want to make a mess in here.'

The man nodded 'You've got balls I'll give you that.'

'Not have when we're done with him.' Commented a man with tattoos across his forearms as he moved outside.

Wath shrugged and looked the leader in the eye. 'Not been using em much recently anyway.'

The man smiled. 'I like you. See you outside.'

Wath nodded and picked up his pint. He emptied it as the last man walked through the door. He stood up, put the empty glass on the bar counter, lifted up the hinged section, walked past Betty, through the bar, through the kitchen and out of the back. As he stepped over the crossing after marching down the hill, he could hear the men starting down the street behind him so instead of going home he went into the signal box and sat down on the floor underneath the window beside the row of levers telling Frank 'Some trouble, just need a minute.'

Three men, lacking their leader, raced around the corner into Treacle Town and started yelling at the end terrace. When nothing happened one of them picked a stone up and threw it through the kitchen window. The glass shattered with a crash and the other men picked up stones and started throwing them at the window.

'Oy! what's going off here!' Jimmy Cotton opened his door and almost fell out. Staggering into the yard he coughed and spluttered, unable to speak as he found his balance.

'He's got it. He's got the flu!' One of the men shouted. 'Get back!' he yelled at Jimmy.

'Bugger you yer little sod' belched Jimmy in as loud a voice as he could 'come here and let me give yer a kiss!'

One by one the men backed away as Jimmy stumbled into the yard. The one with tattooed forearms yelled at the broken window 'We'll get yer Dyson. Just you wait.' Then all three turned and walked away.

Watching the scene unfold beneath him Frank's heart was hammering, his pulse racing as he looked across at Wath who was sat with his back against the wall almost invisible in the semi dark. 'What was all that about?' he asked as Jimmy coughed his way back inside.

'Lucy. Apparently, Henry doesn't want me seeing her and has asked them lot to persuade me.'

55

Frank watched the three men walking back up the hill. All three had broad shoulders and the build of men who knew how to handle themselves.

'What you gunna do? They said they'd be back. Yer can't run away every time.'

'Didn't run away, not from them.' Wath gave a huge sigh and pushed his hair back from his forehead, 'I… I ran away from me, from the man I used to be. I told you I ain't going back to the person I was and I meant it.'

'So, what are yer gunna do then?'

'I'll go see Lucy, ask her to persuade Henry to call em off.'

'And if she doesn't?'

'Then I've got a problem.'

Frank turned to the stove and put the kettle on while Wath rolled, then lit a cigarette.

'Not sure if Lucy will persuade Henry. He's a man who's used to getting his own way.'

By the glow of the cigarette as Wath sucked he saw him shrug his shoulders unconcerned. 'He'll see the light.'

Frank shook his head still agitated. 'I admire your optimism but he's one stubborn man. One who's used to winning and isn't worried about playing dirty!'

'It's ok I can handle him.'

'You think so? He's like a wolf at your throat.'

Wath didn't answer straight away, Frank sensed a reluctance, a doubt about saying anything. But the words came out, softly, quietly as if the incident outside hadn't really happened.

'Ever had a man at your throat?'

'Yeah, fallen out with a few in my time, Not a man like Henry though.'

'No, I mean literally at your throat, biting you, trying to kill you.'

Frank's heart missed a beat. 'No lad, can't say I have.'

Nothing had changed but Frank felt a chill. He could taste a difference in the atmosphere. There was something in Wath's posture, it was as if the events of the night were pushing him backwards and he wasn't resisting.

'It's surreal, outer worldly, a man trying to kill you. Literally every nerve in your body is jumping, screaming.'

Peering into the gloom Frank felt a shift, a change in the conversation away from Henry to somewhere in the past, somewhere real. A blue cloud hung above the corner where Wath sat hidden by the shadows, the whites of his eyes only visible by the reflected light from the coke oven flares. His voice circled within then escaped from the cloud above him with an eerie echoing reverberation. A tone which seemed to date his voice, as if he was speaking from the past with a croak halting each sentence. He was back there revisiting something, seeing it all again.

'He's biting you, trying to rip your throat out, you thrash, you push him off. For an age you roll on the floor, grabbing, punching, squirming, all elbows and knees.'

Frank listened to the words, harsh, brutal, but delivered in a smooth almost tender murmur. He was spellbound as Wath continued.

'Eventually you're locked together. You're staring into his eyes, he's staring into yours, blood running down his chin from where he's been biting you. You head butt him and again, blood spurting from his nose. Still, he looks at you, a furious half mad glare.'

Wath hesitated and then the voice started again, a bell ringing under water. Slow. Deliberate.

'You've managed to get on top, pinning him underneath your body. You've both got knives in your hands but you've got his knife arm pinned with your knee. You pull your knife onto his chest and force the point down. Pushing it through his uniform, through his skin aiming for his heart. The blade slides into his chest, onto a rib and you move it slightly then press harder. You can feel it moving past the rib through his body into his heart.'

57

Frank could feel his own heart beat thumping against his ribs, as he imagined two young men rolling in the mud on the floor of a trench, fighting for survival. The voice droned on strangely unemotional yet Frank felt every syllable, lived every syllable.

'Still, he looks at you. Your faces are only inches apart, you can feel his breath, taste his breakfast, smell his fear. You push the handle of the knife up towards his face then pull it down towards his waist. The blade pivots on his rib bone, slicing his heart.'

Frank stopped breathing, waiting, listening for the echoing voice as Wath pulled on his cigarette, his eyes, painted by the glow of the cigarette, unseeing hollows in his face, a weird red haze replacing the whites, the normally piecing blue iris devoid of colour, lacking feeling, absorbing emotion. He released his next words into the room with the smoke as he exhaled.

'His eyes start to dim but still stare at you. They fade and you watch the life ebb away from them, feel his body relax, still you hold on in case he is faking. Then you can see, see through his eyes into his soul and you know... you know it's over, and you don't even know his name.'

A silence stretched as Frank sat mute unable to think of anything to say. Wath in a deep, deep reverie. Then he started again, still talking as if in a dream.

'You've never felt anything like it, Frank. The adrenalin, the fear, the utter joy of victory. The next few breaths as you lie there bring the most beautiful tasting air your lungs will every breath. There's a buzz running through your body, sheer elation. After a while you want that again. You've been desensitised to your own death, don't care, so you go back for more. More of that ultimate feeling of being alive.' Wath stubbed his cigarette out on the window sill. 'Henry doesn't know what he is taking on. He has no idea.'

Frank watched the dim silhouette, the eyes were now closed, the head tipped back resting against the wall as though he had fought the battle in the last few seconds.

'Thought you weren't gunna talk about the war ever again.'

'I'm not. Technically I haven't'

Frank looked at him confused. He passed a cup of tea over, pulled a cushion onto the floor and sat opposite him. He knew this was his chance, probably his only chance, of the lad opening up to him. 'You've got me now lad.'

Wath sighed.

'After the armistice the Army still had to have some soldiers in France. The Germans had stopped shooting but they still had their guns and no peace treaty had been signed, just an Armistice. We were unlucky, our lot were chosen to stay behind. We'd been at the front and were hardened, just the men the Generals wanted in case it all kicked off again. We were at one end of some burnt out town in the middle of nowhere and the Jerries at the other. We had guns with us and like us theirs were in their barracks. But ten minutes notice and they would be fully armed.'

The drink had greased his throat and the words sounded normal. He was on less intimate, safer ground.

'It was tetchy, an atmosphere between us the like of which you've never experienced. For the past four years we'd been trying to kill them and they'd been trying to kill us. It's all we'd could remember. There were tensions all the time. Arguments were regular, fights were rare but if they happened, they were vicious.

'Anyway, it needed defusing so fights were arranged. If two men crossed each other they would go to a barn a mile outside town and sort it out. The barn was cleared and each man would enter from the side. The other side would supervise him going in, make sure he carried only a knife. Once inside the fighters could only come out through the main door and only one could exit. If the loser was still alive the winner was sent back in. It was brutal but it reduced the tension in the street, every man knew what would happen and what you faced if you caused trouble. At soldier level both sides knew what was happening and would focus on that rather than have the

Ruperts sorting it out. I was a Warrant Officer at the time and supposed to put a stop to it but ignored it.'

Wath stopped, rolled himself another cigarette, marshalling his words. Frank stayed silent. He was deep in his thoughts working through the implications of what Wath had said: Warrant Officer, one down from Captain, the highest rank a non-commissioned officer could attain and yet there was no insignia on the sleeve of his uniform. His thoughts were interrupted as Wath continued his tone changing becoming almost apologetic.

'Then the fights started to be planned, organised, no argument needed, we'll send our man, you send yours. A kind of informal war, organised by the hard men at the bottom. The men who did the dirty stuff in the trenches. Then one of my team didn't come back and the Germans were cock o hoop. Claimed it were an Officer who had done it. So, I volunteered to be next. That were my first time.'

Wath was looking at the floor refusing to make eye contact, his face underlit by the glowing tip of his cigarette, smoke spiralling up his face weaving through his hair before joining the cloud.

'I went into the barn three times more after that. Four times in total. Twice with knives, twice with pick axe handles.'

Frank sat mesmerised. It was said so calmly so bluntly. Four times. Four times the lad in front of him had faced mortal combat. Volunteered for it! Survived it. Fought his enemies and killed them and that after surviving three years in the trenches. Frank didn't have time to process the implications Wath had started talking again.

'The Ruperts got to hear about the barn and panicked. They couldn't afford to have anything escalate, they were trying to set up the occupation of the Rhine, so they transferred us out of France, back to Blighty. Replaced us with new recruits. Youths who'd never seen combat, who'd no axe to grind with the Jerries. But that gave the Generals a problem. They needed fighter's, men who had seen action in case it all started again. So, rather than disband us and send us home they sent us to Clipstone Camp in Nottingham, held us there as reserve, just in case. But the men were only a few miles from home, some of them, me included, had not been home for nearly three years. It was a powder keg just waiting to blow.'

He watched Wath pick something off his trouser leg. Fluff, grit he couldn't see but Wath threw it away. The way he threw it, a bend of the elbow and a flick of the wrist, was an expression of pure frustration.

'It was there that I got a letter from Lucy. They'd been teaching me to read and write so I was dead chuffed. The first letter I would ever read on my own. It was brief. She told me she'd moved out, moved in with some bloke called Henry. I was destroyed, didn't know what to do. I was so close to home, so close to getting back to her and Alice. And she'd gone.

'I was desperate to get back, certain that if I got back in time, I could persuade her to change her mind. I went in and asked when we were going home. We'd just got a new Officer, fresh into service, a man who had never seen mud or blood or bullets, he told me he'd let me know in due course but to remember I was serving King and Country. My head was blown, I was so confused so angry, at Lucy, at Henry, at the Army, at the war. I wanted to scream.'

Frank could hear the pain, the hurt in his voice. There was a huge sigh.

'Anyway, our new Rupert decided to have us parade to keep the men occupied. It was a dismal day, matching my mood, and I couldn't think of anything but Lucy and we're all stood at attention and one of the lads steps out of the line and shouts up 'permission to speak Sir.' Then without waiting for permission he asks loud so everyone can hear 'when can we go home Sir,' It's one of my men Sam Wrightson, he's been with me eighteen months, a real fighter, a man who'd done it all, been at my shoulder many a time. The Rupert walks up to him and snorts through his nose 'Do not speak until you have been given permission soldier. Get back in line.

'Sam just stands there and says 'When Sir?' The Rupert lifts up his parade crop and lashes Sam across the face screaming at him

'Get back.' I don't remember doing it but I ran and threw myself on the Officer ripping him away from Sam, falling onto the ground rolling with him, hitting him with everything I've got.'

Wath raised his head and looked at Frank. Making eye contact for the first time since he started talking.

'Oh, I hit him, bloody hell did I hit him, he was invalided out of the Army after.'

He looked back at the floor and started again. Quicker this time as if he wanted to finish.

'Any way all the Sergeants start to pile in to get me off him and the men threw themselves on the Sergeants. Inside ten seconds there's a full-scale riot. The men out numbered the officers and NCO's and were in the mood for it. Huts were burned, officers beaten up, general mayhem. Other troops and military police were rushed in and order restored.' He gave a huge sigh, 'When it was all over, I was charged with assaulting an officer and starting a riot. They stripped me of my commission and sentenced me to eighteen months imprisonment. Solitary confinement. No contact with the outside world. Took me away to the Glasshouse in Leeds. Got out last Wednesday.'

They sat in silence. The crash of a retort being emptied and wagons being shunted in the pit yard echoed in the distance. Lights flickered across the windows from the coke oven flares. Neither spoke. A bell rang on the panel and Frank got up and pulled the lever. The nine-o clock Barnsley to Doncaster trundled past. Steam from its wheels clouding the windows, smoke from its engine painting them black while the signal box rocked gently to its rhythm. Frank waited until it was past then put the signal back to stop. As he did a service from Wath Hump needed clearance to the main line on route to Immingham. He went through the process of changing signals from one line to the other as the train crossed the tracks of two different companies.

Finally finished he went back to the window. Wath was fast asleep the cup of tea still in his hand, balanced on his knee. Frank removed it, picked his own up then went back to his chair by the stove and picked up his paper. He knew he would not be able to absorb anything yet he didn't want to think about what he'd just heard, what the lad had been through. But he had to. There were demons in the lad's head. Demons which needed trapping and locking away forever. The lad needed his help. He filled a pipe and pulled, blowing the smoke up to the ceiling, the taste was acrid almost acid and burned his mouth but it was just what he wanted right now. It was going to be a long shift.

After an hour Wath stirred, looked up and apologised. 'Sorry, that's the first time that's happened.'

'Nay bother, yer left yer tea, fancy another?'

'Aye.'

As Frank mashed the tea, he heard Wath getting comfortable again and lighting another cigarette. The lad was still wanting to talk. 'I don't sleep well, you know.'

Frank passed him his drink and sat back on the cushion on the floor opposite him. 'Not really surprising is it, with what you've been through.' Frank could only assume that tonight Wath was getting things off his chest, cleansing himself, or trying to justify in his own mind his actions of the past few hours. The contrast between this evening and his memories could not have been starker. But this was a new Wath, a Wath trying to come to terms with his past and Frank had never seen this far inside the lad. It was an unsettling experience. Wath waited for him to relax then continued.

'If I lie down, I have the same dream every time.' Again, he hesitated, picking his words unsure how to describe what he saw.

'In the dream I'm laid in a field, there's meadow grass and daisies and dandelions and buttercups and corn flowers. And poppies lots of poppies. It's morning and I have to get up but there's a mist. It's a low mist and it starts to cover the field. I sit up so I'm above the mist and the suns out trying to burn the mist off.'

Wath sipped the hot tea and nodded. Frank wasn't sure if he nodded at the tea or the memory.

63

'But as I start to get to my feet, I realise it's not a mist. Its ghosts. Hundreds and hundreds of ghosts all lying on the ground around me. They're all men. Men I've killed. Men who've died at my side. Men I don't know. Men I do. Men who marched out of England with me. Men who marched from Germany to meet me. Hundreds and hundreds of them and they are all looking at me asking why am I not yet dead. And I look up towards the sun. Its glowing bright and at its side hanging in the sky is the moon except it's not a moon and it's not still. It's a bullet and its spinning and coming towards me, straight for me and I know it's got my name on and it's coming and coming, getting larger and larger. Then, just before it hits, I wake up.'

They both drank their tea, neither knowing what to say until Wath said.

'So, I sleep in a chair, I never lie down.

'I hide from ghosts.'

Chapter Eight

Sunday 22/2/1920

Wath stayed with Frank until the end of his shift then walked back home. There was glass all over the kitchen. He picked the big pieces up first then swept the smaller ones into a bucket. Taking it all outside he threw it into the middle of the main line where the trains would crush it to dust.

On his return Jimmy was waiting for him.

'You alright lad?' he wheezed.

'Fine. Thanks for last night.'

'No bother. Who were they?'

'Just some fellas wanting to give me a love bite.'

'I must be damn ugly then cos they didn't want mine.'

Wath smiled 'Yer looking better though.'

'Aye I'm over the worst of it. Back to normal in a couple of days.'

'Good to know. Best get back, got some tiding up to do. Can I borrow your tool kit?'

Once back inside Wath assessed the damage. The window was virtually glassless. Opening the sashes, he unscrewed the hinges and removed them. Going outside he used a claw hammer to prise the corrugated steel off the window next door. Forcing the window open he removed its opening sashes and taking them back used them to replace his broken old windows which he shoved through into the kitchen next door before boarding up the window again. After admiring his handy work, he went inside and had a breakfast of bread and cheese.

There was nothing left to do and it being a Sunday he reasoned even Mallinder's thugs would take the day off so he set about washing his clothes as best he could. Scrubbing the dirt from his shirts he considered how he could keep his word to himself and not resort to violence. It had been the biggest part of his life for so long that he struggled to think how he could settle any issue without taking matters into his hands, hands curled into fists. No matter how hard it was he had to try, he needed a normal life. He wanted Lucy and Alice back to give him the stability, the responsibility of normality. But he was certain Henry would send his men again. If he did, Wath needed to be ready. He needed to plan for the worst.

He screwed as much water as possible from the shirts. Leaving them to dry he walked alongside the tracks through the sidings and into Wath Main wood yard. The security man looked worried but Wath approached him and asked if there were any old pick axe handles going. After a negotiation Wath paid sixpence for two old handles and returned home.

Standing one behind the door he spent some time forcing a metal rail tie inside the split head of the second before tightly wrapping it in canvas sacking. Then he dipped the canvas covered head into bitumen ripped from the side of a salt store alongside the tracks and warmed in a broken old bucket. Apart from the dark head it looked much the same as any handle but there was more weight in the business end. He tested it for balance a few times.

Just before closing time, he tucked the handle under his jacket, holding it flat against his side with his arm and walked up to the Nelson. As was her custom Betty had pulled all the curtains shut to stop passer-by's looking in, indicating service was over. The locals were inside finishing their pints before leaving. After a quick survey of the area Wath strode in through the open outer doors, turned and placed the handle on the shelf at the back of and above the outer door. Pushing it to the rear so it could not be seen he rechecked the inner doors were closed, the frosted glass hiding him from those inside. In less than four seconds he was back outside and strolling back home.

Satisfied, a long day ended with him reading his book and hanging sheets across the window before he slept. If the four men

66

did return, he did not want to be surprised by shards of glass showering over him.

Betty pulled the pint and passed it over. There was an atmosphere inside the bar she couldn't quite put her finger on. The usual team was in, Bill, Syd, Tom and Ted all playing dominoes while the two young lads Walt and Jack were at the bar watching her figure closely as she pulled pints. Last night they all witnessed four men threaten a regular and watched him run away. It was what they would all do in the same circumstances but for some reason it did not sit well. After three years pulling pints in the same room, she could feel the changed mood but was at a loss to describe it.

Bill from the domino team was the first to raise it. It was always Bill. 'Well, that were entertaining last night. He's a right piece o work that Mallinder. Didn't like the look of his lads neither.' He slapped double three onto the table with a look of pure glee.

Syd scowled and knocked, tapping the table unable to play a domino. 'He's plain nasty and bloody arrogant if yer asks me. If young Wath had been beaten up we'd all be witnesses.'

'Aye' Bill said 'but would yer say owt with them four prowling?'

Syd ignored the question and ploughed on. 'I were surprised he ran though. He must have seen worse than that in the trenches.'

Tom placed his domino with infinite care as if he were placing a two-penny stamp on an envelope and making sure the sides of the stamp corresponded with the sides of the envelope. 'Nobody likes a thrashing.' He commented settling back to admire his handiwork. No one was fooled they all knew he had blocked that end of the board and that his comments were as much about dominoes as last night's episode.

'He's already had a few thrashings looking at his face.' Bill gave a slight nod towards Syd.

Syd knocked again and growled. 'Shunt have run though. He'll be branded a coward for that.'

The youngsters at the bar had been listening and it was too much for Walt. 'I tell yer he's no coward, he's done more than most. Got medals.'

'What sprint medals?'

'Bugger off Syd, me dad says he's an hero.'

'Think you'll have to make that "was an hero" he weren't no hero last night.'

In desperation Walt turned to Betty for support. 'What do you think Betty?'

'I think he was right to run and if you want a coward then Mallinder's yer man. Couldn't do it himself so he brings four men to beat him up. Four!'

Syd pulled his pint from the shelf under the table. 'Aye odds were a bit steep but he shunt have run.'

Walt stood up. 'What would you have done then mouth almighty?'

'Taken me beating like a man. Get it over and done with. Mark my word they'll be back now they know he's a coward.'

'He int no coward.' Walt bawled, hammering his pint onto the counter 'I'll prove it to yer.' and raced out of the pub.

'Looks like he's got a bee in his bonnet, are yer going to play that bloody domino Bill or do we have to sit here all night?'

Bill slammed the domino on the table. 'I would have run.'

Ted waved his empty glass at Betty and spoke for the first time. 'I like the lad; he's been decent company and he keeps himself to himself when the times right. But Syd's got a point, I didn't think of it like that. I would have run, but they'll be back, he's gunna have to take his beating some time or another.'

Betty turned back to the bar and pulled Tom another pint, young Jack was sat with an empty glass and Walt's half-finished pint at the side of him. 'Want another?' she asked.

'Yeah, but it's his round,' nodding at Walt's glass 'can you put it on his tab?'

'Bloody cheapskate. Yeh, okay. What's he doing? Where's he gone?'

'Don't know but if he's not back before I finish this, I'm having the rest of his pint.'

'Cheapskate!'

The rattle of the dominos returned as the team shuffled for a new hand and a peaceful calm enveloped the bar, all the occupants thinking their own thoughts about last night.

'Do yer think he'll come back?' Betty asked out loud to no one in particular. Syd replied.

'Who? Wath, not if he's got any sense, not until Henry's called off his dogs.'

To muffled laughs Betty announced 'Looks like I'll never get that Mackeson!'

They all turned back to their beers and dominos. Jack finished his pint and moved Walt's across in front of him. Looking at Betty with a grin he shrugged his shoulders and took a drink. Two minutes later the door burst open and Walt fell inside gasping for breath waving bits of paper in his hand.

'Here, here' he yelled 'told you he was an hero.' He walked across to the domino table and slapped newspaper cuttings into the middle disturbing several dominoes.

'Oye! careful yer stupid young bugger.' The team all threw their arms up, cursed and moaned mightily, gesticulating furiously until the dominoes where back in place. Bill thumped the next domino onto the line then looked at Walt. 'What yer got there then?'

'Paper cuttings from when he got his medals, me dad kept em.'

'Well, read em out then.'

Walt was still getting his breath back. 'You read em.'

'I ent got me glasses.'

Syd laughed. 'He can't read lad, you read em, it'll save time.'

69

Walt grabbed the cuttings and went to the bar. 'I need a pint after that sprint.'

'Your round' said Jack 'I'll have another while you're at it.' Betty looked at him sideways. Picking up his fresh beer Walt sat at the side of the domino table, Jack and Betty shuffled along the bar to be closer.

'Okay. Here's the first one.'

'*Military Medal. For repeated reconnaissance's under heavy fire, gaining valuable information and maintaining efficient communications throughout a period of several days. He was most unselfish throughout and cheerful at all times and under all circumstances.*'

'Huh. He gets a medal for that. After Treacle Town he must have thought he was staying at the Hilton.'

'Syd, shut up, let him read.'

'*Distinguished Conduct Medal. For conspicuous gallantry and devotion to duty under close enemy machine-gun fire. The attack on Faubourg de Paris being held up by heavy machine-gun fire, he went forward with four men. The four men became casualties, he went on by himself and, showing an utter disregard for danger, launched a counter-attack which was successful.*'

'What he's a one-man army now, exaggeration that is.'

'For Christs sake Syd shut up and let the lad read.' The game of dominos was forgotten.

'*Military Cross. For conspicuous gallantry and devotion to duty as NCO in charge during an attack on the Hindenburg Line north of Bellicourt, although enemy machine gun and shell fire were intense this officer took forward two teams and in vicious hand to hand fighting succeeded in removing two guns.*'

Walt placed the cuttings down and looked at his audience triumphantly. There was a lull then they all started at once.

'Officer! Nowt were said about him being an Officer.'

'Did it say hand to hand combat?'

'Yeh.'

'Bloody hell, that's fucking frightening.'
'Two guns! Do they mean two machine guns?'
'It don't say, but I don't think they mean pistols.'
'Jesus.'
'So **why** did he run?'

Chapter Nine

Friday 27/2/1920

The next few days passed in a blur as Wath started his new job. Joe Whiteley was a good man and the delivery round he gave Wath was reasonable. That was if Wath could get Jewel on his side. Jewel was a stubborn horse and did not like change so having Wath as her new master did not go down well. 'Apples' Joe told him 'she likes apples.' After a couple of days bribing the horse things started to ease and she and Wath settled into a comfortable routine.

It felt good having responsibility for the horse and every day he spent an hour after their rounds making sure she had enough feed and giving Jewel a rub down and brush. Joe was meticulous in his treatment of the horse. Feed was supplemented with molasses and despite there being no evidence of any Jewel was sprayed with flea powder every week. She was fit and strong and good natured. If she liked you.

Walking home on the Friday he realised he had fed the horse but not himself. Not feeling like cooking he decided upon fish and chips. Leaving Lockwood's to be his final destination he entered the Lord Nelson for the first time since Saturday and ordered a pint. Betty served him with a look on her face he could not fathom. Ignoring it he sat under the window and watched the team playing dominoes. They all nodded to him but no one said anything. He could see that they all wanted to question him but weren't bold enough to ask. Shrugging internally, he left them to it and savoured his pint. He was only half way down it when the door opened and Lucy walked in. The dominoes stopped for a minute as the men all appraised her, then started again with a muted click clack as they watched her every movement. Wath sat motionless.

At the bar Lucy ordered two pints and Betty pulled them, the look on her face one of pure jealousy as she took in Lucy's expensive hat and coat. Picking up the two pints Lucy left the bar and placing both pints on the table in front of Wath said. 'Mind?' pointing at the chair opposite him. He gestured for her to sit down and she pushed a pint in front of him. Lifting the other one she raised her glass with a nod of cheers then took a decent pull, replaced the glass and sighed.

'God. That's the only thing I miss about Treacle Town, a decent pint.'

He smiled and looked at her. 'What's wrong with the beer in the Red Lion or the New Inn?'

'Henry thinks "Ladies" should drink delicate drinks you know be sophisticated.'

'Such as?'

'Martini, that's what he likes me to drink.'

'What does Martini taste like?'

'Toothpaste.' She looked up quickly, examining him 'you do know what toothpaste tastes like, don't you?'

'Yeah... Martini.'

They both laughed out loud. She dug into her purse and pulled out a packet of cigarettes. Marlborough. She examined the label. 'American, he must think they're sophisticated.' Taking one for herself she offered him one from the packet. 'Go on. Henry paid for them.'

He offered her a light then lit his, pulling hard. The tube shrank half an inch and he couldn't taste a thing. She smiled noting his expression. 'Doesn't cut through the coke ovens fog, does it?'

'Nah. What're doing here Lucy?'

She took a pull on the Marlborough before answering 'Come to tell you I've had a word with Henry. I heard about the other night. Wanted to tell you I had nothing to do with it. Knew nothing about it. I've told him to stop.' Blowing her smoke at him she added 'If I want to hurt you, I'll do it myself.'

73

He smiled and nodded in agreement 'And will he?'

'Says so.'

'How did you hear? Henry tell you?'

'No. Frank. He came up to the house when Henry was at work. Told me what happened. Told me he thought you'd changed. That walking away was the bravest thing you could've done.'

'He's always had too high an opinion o me.'

She smiled 'Tells me you've got a job.'

'Aye, honest employment.'

'There's a thing hey. Any way I wanted to tell you myself, that way messages don't get messed up.'

'Thank you. Want another.'

'No, got to go.'

'Can I see Alice?'

'Leave it with me Wath. Give me and Henry time. Let us get used to you being back.'

He nodded 'Okay but not too long. Let me know.'

Standing up, she nodded in agreement. 'Look after yourself.' She turned and left.

The domino table went silent again as they watched her leave. Lucy gave them a little wave and smile as Betty followed her every step from the bar with a miserable glare.

Bill leant across from the domino table. 'Don't know what you've got lad, what with Betty drooling over you and rich beauties coming in and buying you beers, but whatever it is, can I buy some?'

'Bill I've no idea, and even if I did,' he said grinning, 'I wouldn't sell it.' He looked to the bar where Betty was sat waiting for more orders with a frown on her face.

'Betty, can I have another pint please and while you're at it can you pour yourself that Mackeson, I promised you.'

Chapter Ten

Saturday 28/2/1920

The next day after he finished his deliveries Wath walked back through town and stopped at the Chemists. There was all kinds of potions and bottles on display behind glass counters and Wath was left confused by the so-called organisation. Seeking out the assistant he asked for toothpaste.

'Do you want a brush as well?'

'Sorry?'

'A brush, do you need one as well?'

Wath looked vacantly at the assistant. 'You know to brush your teeth using the toothpaste.'

'Oh yeah, sorry I was miles away.'

Taking his purchases back home Wath read the instructions and put a pea sized piece of toothpaste on his new brush and scrubbed his teeth. All he could think was if that was what Martini tasted like there was no wonder Lucy was necking pints in three swallows.

After the prescribed two minutes he rinsed his mouth out with water surprised to see blood. There was something wrong here but he wasn't sure what. Was this the way forward? His old home-made tooth powder made with salt and baking soda rubbed in with his finger seemed to work but after the toothpaste he could not stop licking his teeth which he acknowledged felt clean and fresh.

Leaving a stew to bubble in the pot he went for a pint and nearly choked on the first mouthful. It tasted so different. He was starting to doubt this sophistication but the look on Lucy's face had convinced him that he should try.

He sat musing, trying to take the taste away with a cigarette, when Bill leant over.

'Another woman's been asking after you.'

'What're yer on about?'

'I went into Kate's shop earlier and there was a woman in, never seen her before, and she was asking where you lived.'

'Nay you've got that wrong.'

'No, she definitely asked about you. There was only the young girl on and she just said "I think he lives in Treacle Town.".'

'So, what did you say?'

'Nowt, you've got enough woman trouble as it is!'

As Wath crossed the railway lines on his way home Frank leant out of the window of the signal box and waved. Running up the steps he pushed in as Frank let the ten-o clock service through on the GCR line.

'How's the job?' Frank asked pulling levers and watching the flags on the panel.

'Great. Didn't think I'd be this happy in honest work but Joe's a good bloke and, providing I have an apple in mi pocket, me and the horse is getting on fine.' Wath's tone turned negative as he shook his head. 'Got to tell you it'll not last forever though. I watched a lorry delivering to Wards today and it did the job in half the time me and Jewel could do it in and it carried twice as much stuff. Joe's got to move with the times and get lorries.'

'He's too long in the tooth to change.'

'Yeah, I know, but I feel like I'm always behind the times. First the barges when they were out of date now a horse and cart when lorries are beating us to the work.'

'So, what you gunna do?'

'Oh, I'll stick with it, enjoying it too much, but it can't last.'

Frank finished with the levers and looked across trying to read Wath's face.

'Fred tells me there's been a woman knocking on your door this morning.'

'Aye?'

'Yeah, you was out and Jimmy's gone back to work so she didn't get a reply.'

'Who was it?'

'Fred didn't know her or the bloke with her but he says she shouted up here and asked for you. He said you was at work and to try the Nelson later.'

Wath shook his head in frustration. 'I've no idea who it could be.'

'Never mind if it's important she'll find yer.'

Chapter Eleven

Friday 5/3/1920

The following Friday Wath had deliveries in Mexborough so tethering Jewel outside he had himself measured for a suit in Burtons, the assistant seemed more interested in talking about the probability of strike action by the miners rather than his new outfit. Listening with only half an ear Wath learned that the railway workers and dockers would join the strike. Not wanting to encourage the assistant too much as he had to get back quickly, he tried to decipher how this would affect Frank. But it appeared the assistant's information came from miners grumbling in his shop and he had no information on the railways. Agreeing a rate for a suit, a pair of trousers and three new shirts he depleted his reserves but was comfortable knowing he had a wage coming in. The trousers needed a little adjustment so he arranged to pick them up the next day.

Saturday 6/3/1920

With his second wage packet in his pocket on the Saturday Wath had a shower at the public baths, bought a pair of second-hand shoes from the cobblers and picked up his new clothes. Determined to get on top of his tooth brush he fought his way through brushing his teeth and dressed in his new clothes. Feeling like a different person he strode out to the Lord Nelson.

As he entered there were wolf whistles from the domino table while Betty could not contain her smile. Pulling his pint, she asked provocatively

'Is all that effort for me? Cos if it is it's working!'

78

Sitting at his usual seat he rolled himself a cigarette as Walt and Jack entered. They ordered pints than moved across and sat next to him.

'What's going off then? You got a date?'

Smiling he ignored the banter and settled in comfortably.

Bill leant across from the dominoes. 'She were here last night looking for yer.'

'Who?' Wath's heart jumped at the thought Lucy had been back.

'That woman from the shop. Came in here with a bloke asking about yer.'

Covering his disappointment, he said 'Frank told me someone called at the house while I was working.'

Syd piped up 'Yer'd best get him under yer spell quick Betty lass, he's got more women after him than you can shake a stick at.'

'I'm not worried about her from last night Syd, too old for him. Yer don't like older women... do yer Wath?'

Syd was on a roll. 'Aye but she was bonnie though, yer'll have to agree.'

'Calm down yer randy bugger, I'll be telling Mary.'

Grins erupted all around but everyone looked at Wath as Bill asked 'So who is she then?'

'Keep telling yer I've no idea.'

'Well, I'll tell yer lad, in truth she was a bit old for you but she was a good looker. If yer fancy lending me some o that charm yer've got I'll stop her bothering yer.'

The evening collapsed into gentle mickey taking before Wath said goodnight and made to exit. As he left his glass on the bar Betty leant across. 'It's my day off tomorrow I fancy a walk and a change of scenery. Fancy joining me?'

'Where to?'

'Just into town, they've got a brass band playing in front of the Town Hall, be different, then we can call at the Saracens for a pint.'

'Go on then.'

'I'll meet you at Gore Hill Bridge at ten.'

'Ok.' Wath had not taken four strides down the street when he heard the cheer from the domino table. Betty hadn't wasted any time telling them.

Chapter Twelve

Sunday 7/3/1920

The following morning freshly scrubbed and suited, Wath met
Betty at the bridge and they walked into the town centre. There was
a temporary bandstand behind the Town Hall with seats in front but
nothing had started as everyone was in Church for the Sunday
Service. Wath and Betty had a slow stroll through Newhill Park then
returned to see the chairs almost full and the band starting up.
Parking themselves at the back of the seats they settled down to
listen. Betty was enthralled. But for Wath the uniforms and precise
marching tunes irked reminding him too much of the Military and it
took some concentration to sit as if enjoying the performance.

Throughout he could feel eyes on him as a ripple passed through
the audience when they realised who he was. Feeling uncomfortable
under the scrutiny, as soon as the band finished, he said 'come on
let's have that pint.' But before they could move out of the line of
chairs, he noticed Lucy standing up at the front with Alice alongside
her and Henry talking to another man. Lucy looked across, took in
his new suit and appearance seeming to appreciate the change. She
made a nodding sign with her head indicating the side of the seating.
She had a quick word with Henry then steered Alice towards the
side. Betty watched the movement through narrowed eyes.

Wath turned to Betty 'Give me a minute.'

'I'm coming with you.' She declared in a tone that brooked no
argument.

Wath gave her a rigid stare and said 'No. You are not. Give me a
minute Betty. I'll be back before you know it.'

Moving alongside Lucy he looked at Alice who was dressed
impeccably with her blonde hair tied in a long pigtail.

'Hi.' Said the young girl.

'Hi. You look great.'

'Ta. Do them marks on your face hurt?'

'Alice no—'

'—No, no it's ok Lucy, honest. No Alice not now, they don't hurt anymore.'

'You were in the war weren't you'

'Yes.'

'Ok. Did you read your book?'

'Not yet, been busy – working. Did you read yours?'

'Yeah, course, had two more since then.'

The girl then started to lose interest and looked around. Wath turned his attention to Lucy.

'Any news? Can I see her?'

'Henry's not happy.' They looked across and could see Henry scowling in their direction, 'but give me another couple of weeks and I'll have him persuaded.'

He grinned 'That would be great.'

'Your friend doesn't look too happy either.' Wath looked over his shoulder at where Betty stood at the back of the seats fuming.

'Yeah, they'd make a great couple wouldn't they.'

Lucy burst out laughing which turned Henry and Betty's frowns even deeper. Wath couldn't help but join in.

'Got to say you look a lot smarter than you did at the library.'

'Yeah, working has its benefits.'

'Look, I'll speak with you when I've got Henry convinced but let's leave it for now. See you later.'

Wath watched her every step as she walked away then returned to Betty.

'I thought you was with me today!' she stormed.

'Betty that's my daughter I'm trying to see her more often.'

'Did you know *she* would be here?'

'No! Remember it was your idea.'

'Yeah right. You can forget that pint. I'm going home.'

82

Chapter Thirteen

Friday 12/3/1920

The week passed with a pattern developing as Jewel welcomed Wath in a morning and pulled the cart with gusto. When Friday came Wath was once again delivering in Mexborough. Jewel had just pulled her own weight in coal uphill for four miles and needed a blow so Wath stopped and stood by her head feeding her an apple and giving her a drink from the water trough at the side of the road.

There was a chugging noise and a lorry pulled up opposite. It was from Thrybergh Bottom Pit. Two men climbed out of the passenger side and jumped on the back of the flat bed. There were half a dozen metal boxes there which they lifted down and carried into the bank.

As the vehicle was unattended Wath walked across and looked into the cab. Both the doors were only half doors with no glass in the top half and the driver's door was welded closed. Inside the cab the pedals were the same as the army lorries he had travelled in, the steering wheel and the gear lever all looked very similar. He was still looking in when the two men walked out of the Bank shouting over their shoulder that they would be back next week. Wath moved to one side as they climbed in and the driver shuffled across.

'You alright?' he asked Wath, a suspicious look etched on his face.

'Yeh, just looking at the lorry, that's my cart over there and I'm trying to persuade my boss to buy one of these.' he replied pointing at the lorry 'What is it?'

'A Leyland P, best little motor you can get, but he'd best have some brass your gaffer, eight hundred pounds each these little beauties. Good luck.'

He pulled away from the curb and within seconds was doing twenty miles an hour. Wath shook his head. Jewel could only do that at top speed and only for a hundred yards or so even without the cart. He looked back at the bank and resolve came over him. Walking in he stood and waited for a counter to come clear then asked the cashier how to get a loan. He pointed him to another man who came and sat at a table offering him the other chair.

'Right so you want a loan.'

Trying not to be intimidated by the officious manner of the man before him Wath answered, 'Please, I want to persuade my boss to buy a lorry, he'll need eight hundred pounds. So, I thought I'd come in and ask for the details, so I can get him to do it.'

'Sorry but I can only talk to your boss. I can only advise the person sat in front of me. If you were after the loan, it would be different.'

Wath looked at the man, he was only after information, what was so hard about that 'Well, what if I want a loan then?'

'Ah, that is different, do you have a bank account?'

'No.'

'Do you own a house or have a rent book?'

'No.'

'Do you have a contract for the work this lorry will carry out.'

'No. I work for Mr Whiteley, he has the contract.'

'Ok, do you have a wage slip from Mr Whiteley?'

'No, he pays me cash.'

'Therefore, you have no security or assets to underpin a loan. These are all things I must have to calculate the loan, unfortunately without these I cannot estimate the risk or cost of a loan.'

'Will he need to have these things? Cos he'll get the work and pay you back.'

'No doubt but if he doesn't where do I go to find him?' the man sighed an exasperated sigh, 'Yes he will need all these things and then and only then can I advise him of the cost. Look we currently charge five percent interest but without speaking to your boss I don't know how long the loan will be for or what to use for security. I'm sorry but you really need Mr Whiteley to come in. Sorry.'

He stood up, shook Wath's hand in a hand shake that would have struggled to make an impression in a bowl of jelly and disappeared behind the counter. A chastened Wath went back to Jewel and started back to the stables. He would have to push Joe harder - lorries were the only way forward.

Back at the stables Wath was brushing Jewel when Joe walked in. Wath went straight on the attack as Joe stood shaking head.

'Boss, I know you're not keen but over the past few days I've seen lorries delivering coal, cement, fruit and veg and even money boxes. I know, I know, but they all do it faster than me and Jewel and if you can borrow eight hundred pounds, we can get one and do twice as much. All you've g—' Before Wath could go any further Joe held up his hand,

'Wath calm down, take it easy. They'll be no lorry. I'm sorry lad but I'm going to have to let you go.'

'Eh… Why?'

'Henry Mallinder's threatened to take his sand supply contract from me if you carry on working for me. Sorry lad, here's your wages up to date. I've enjoyed working with you but I can't take on Henry Mallinder.' There was a long period of silence as both men looked at each other. Joe pushed his hand forward again. 'Sorry.' Wath felt his world shrink as he shook Joe's hand, took the envelope, stroked Jewel and walked out.

Back at Treacle Town Wath made himself a cup of tea and sat in front of the fire, his temper on a slow burn. Somehow, he had to find another job and worse still he had to tell Frank. Pondering this a knock on the door made him jump and spill his tea, burning his chin. He wiped the mess with his sleeve before shouting 'Come in.'

Constable Goulding walked in with another local policeman, PC Hopewell from Avenue Road.

'Yeah?' a surprised Wath asked.

'Where were you last Sunday morning?' Goulding demanded.

Wath stared at the policeman wanting to be careful with his answer, uncertain of where this was going.

'Newhill Park then the Town Hall to watch the band. Why?'

'I know where you were at the Town Hall it's before then I want to know about. Which way did you walk?'

'High Street then Cemetery Road. What's going off here?' he asked Hopewell.

'A member of the congregation was pick pocketed before the Sunday Service, you were seen in the area and we know your reputation.'

'Weren't me.'

'So, you say, where did you get them new clothes?' Goulding said pointing to the new suit, trousers and shirts hanging from the picture rail.

'I paid for them.'

'Aye but who's money did you use? Mind if we have a look around?'

Wath made a sweeping gesture, there wasn't much to see.

Goulding moved through the other rooms while Hopewell inspected the sideboard at the back of the room. He pulled out the receipts from Winfield and Burtons.

'Goulding' he called 'The lads got receipts for them clothes, bought them before Sunday and paid for them by selling his medals.'

Goulding stormed into the room and grabbed the receipts reading them slowly. He lifted his eyes, anger smouldering.

'Not happy, you were in the vicinity and witnesses say you looked shifty.'

Suddenly it all dropped into place.

'It were Mallinder weren't it. He's blamed me and you're just his lap dogs.'

'Now, now lad let's not get like that.' Hopewell cautioned 'You know we can't tell you who told us.'

'Yeah, but you'd deny it if it weren't him' his patience was now at its limit 'have you done here cos you're spoiling me cup of tea.'

Goulding stood as close as he possibly could to Wath. 'This is your last warning. Any more trouble and I'll beat the living day light's out of you.'

'Yeah, sticks and stones Goulding. Get him out of here.' He said to Hopewell and turned back to his chair and his tea.

Later he walked up to the signal box and stood by the window, rolling a cigarette, while waiting for Frank to sort out the six thirty to Wombwell.

'Got some bad news,' he started 'Joe's laid me off, Henry's threatened to cancel his contract if he keeps me on and Joe can't afford to lose that.'

Frank looked disbelieving, 'But that's wrong, that's just not right.'

'Yeah, but that's how it works. He didn't stop there either. He shopped me to the police for pick pocketing last Sunday while I was with Betty. Don't worry I didn't do it.'

'Jesus Wath, he's after you. What have you done?'

'As far as I know absolutely nothing, but he can't stand me being near Lucy.'

'So, what are you going to do?'

'Look for a job.'

'Unemployment's setting records, everybody going on strike, layoffs everywhere. Bloody hell this is crap.'

'Yeah, but it's just the way it is, big fish feed on the little fish, it'll never stop.'

'Mallinder is nasty.'

'He's no different to the rest.'

'Not everybody is like him.'

'You'd be surprised.'

'Go on then surprise me.'

Wath took a long hard pull of his cigarette and considered Frank over the top of the smoke. This would be taking trust to a whole

87

new level. He considered the cost and decided Frank knew enough anyway, a little more wouldn't hurt.

'Remember when the lead was stolen from the church roof?'

'Yeah. There were a right uproar'

'Well, that were me. It were a right job but I got it all down and took it in a barrow to Jonny Elgin. Sold him the lot at his scrap yard. Took several trips and he knew where everyone came from. The same Jonny Elgin who has a pew on the front row of the church.'

'I remember, wait didn't his m—'

'Yeah, his Missus complained cos the roof leaked and she got wet. Jonny had to contribute to have the roof mended. Tried to get his contribution back off me. Huh as if.'

There was no point holding back now, he had opened the dam and Frank was going to find out just how trustworthy and honest the gentle folk of Wath upon Dearne really were.

'They're all the same Frank. Remember when Smiths shop went up in flames? Yeah? That were me. Paid to torch it. Paid by Percy Shaw Jnr… that's right the honourable upstanding Percy Shaw Jnr whose family has had their own pew in the church for over two hundred years. He owned the building and had it insured. He knew Smith had over insured his stock and would get the blame. He did and was sent down for fraud and arson. That's right, the Wilfred Smith who argued his innocence in court till he was blue in the face and still got sent down. The Wilfred Smith whose wife got thrown in the workhouse. The wife who was on the same church fundraising group as Shaw's missus. Shaw sat and watched it all, got the pay out, rebuilt the shop better, went into partnership with his cousin Sam Cudworth who ran it for them and they both made a fortune while paying Shaw a bigger rent.

'All of them church goers, all of them pillars of society, all of them crooks. Henry's no different. This is just personal with him.'

Wath studied Frank's face. He could see he was having a hard time accepting this.

'Easiest was when I did ten burglaries for Stuart Netheridge, two of them on his own sites, he even left me the keys. The rest were cover so it looked like he was just another victim and could claim from the insurance.

'And that's nowhere near the full list, I could keep going Frank but you've got the gist. Back then they all knew me. They all hated me and near on all used me. You should've seen the looks on Sunday when I turned up at their Brass Band with Betty. I reckon half the congregation had panic attacks, at least two thirds of the front row and all of the bloody Masons.'

Frank shook his head in disbelieve. 'So, what are you going to do?'

Jimmy Cotton was stood in the yard waving at the signal box.

'Right now, I'm going for a pint with Jimmy. I need a long think but I tell you a lorry's the answer. I've got to find some way to get a lorry. I were trying to get Joe to buy one but that's gone now. There must be a way, must be someone I can borrow the money off cos I'm certain that's the way forward.'

'What about Goulding?' Frank asked as Wath reached the door.

'He can't do a thing unless I do summat daft. He's no worry.'

'What about Mallinder?'

'I've told you. I don't want to go back to the man I was Frank and I meant it. But if Henry pushes too hard...' He closed the door behind him.

Chapter Fourteen

Saturday 13/3/1920

Saturday was a long day as Wath sat immersed in his thoughts. His opportunity to make a fresh start in life had been ripped from him. It was the same old story. Every single time an opportunity presented itself something somehow took it away.

The army had forced discipline on him, added the ability to read and write but also taught him skills he wanted to forget. He wanted the normal everyday life some people took for granted.

It had been folly to buy the new clothes. His funds were now seriously depleted. He could live off little, there was only him and he paid no rent. His funds would last him three or four possibly even five weeks if he limited his drinking. But he needed to find work. The chance to make money.

He smiled, it was difficult to make money legally when your whole life was lived on the edge. The bosses, the owners, the men in charge thought little of their workers. They were simply replaceable muscle and no one wanted a worker with his reputation. He thought of all the businessmen in the area, there were few he respected, he could not think of one who had made their money legitimately unless it was handed down to them. Then, he reasoned, it must have been their parents who trod the wrong side of the line.

He worried all day and by nightfall was no further forward. But as he sat in the chair watching the flames in the fire grate an idea started to take shape in his mind. Unable to sleep Wath left the house at midnight.

The idea was beginning to make sense.

It was burning, a low flame which would not go out. But if there was to be any substance to the idea, he needed to be sure, to fully understand the movements of the trains in the early hours.

Picking up his mother's pocket watch and a full water bottle he marched down the tracks taking the colliery curve to the Midland line then following it past the Adwick crossing to the bridge over Mexborough Road where the Midlands and North East Railway and Midland lines joined. Sitting down on the bridge he watched the signals from the other lines move up and down as they prepared for the next day.

Traffic on the main lines was slow during the night and the collieries tended to concentrate on filling their wagons ready for onward shipment the following morning. In the distance an internal shunt engine was busy shuffling wagons in the sidings but that was all inside the colliery yard and Wath could only hear the movement.

There was a pile of old sleepers by the side of the bridge wall and pulling his coat tight he settled himself against them watching and waiting.

After a long spell of inactivity, he checked his watch, it was still only four am and rail traffic was virtually non-existent. An over-night sleeper trundled past heading for Edinburgh and he watched the signals change then revert back. Wath meticulously timed its movement and the changing of the signals.

He waited another hour then returned home and fried himself eggs before catching up with his sleep.

When Frank arrived at the signal box, he went to see him and spent an hour pouring over the train timetables.

'What're looking for?' asked Frank.

'Not sure' he replied 'the patterns don't seem the same as when I was last here. Fewer movements in the night, not that I'm complaining like, get more sleep, but unless I'm mistaken the MNER line has more traffic than it used to.'

'Yeah, the spurs to Leeds and Bradford are more popular and competing well with the east coast line up to Edinburgh through Newcastle.'

Wath turned back to the time tables and Frank watched him, amused at how serious he was about the train services. He may have

91

been to war but his curiosity and thirst for knowledge hadn't diminished.

After a while Wath put the timetable down, said goodbye and left Frank. Back home he rifled through his mother's sideboard, found an old pencil and an unused diary and made notes. Slipping the diary into his pocket he walked up the GCR line to Wath Station. He then crossed to the Midland line following that back down to the colliery curve. Choosing that branch, he followed it to the MNER line before taking that back to the GCR line just outside Mexborough to where it joined the colliery lines at Wath Junction. By walking alongside this he returned to Treacle Town having completed a full circuit of the lines and tracks which surrounded the terrace.

Pulling out the largest piece of paper he could find, Winfield's receipt, he consulted his notes and made a sketch of the layout marking the signals and junctions.

He then spent the afternoon sat at Hound Hill bridge on the MNER line recording the timings of the signal changes.

The following week he walked Wath upon Dearne on Monday and Mexborough on Wednesday looking for work. The other days of the week, he walked the tracks, leaving the weekends free.

On Thursday he repeated his overnight vigil on Adwick bridge. Once again, the overnight sleeper was on time at four-o clock. The only other movement was a pit lorry rattling under the bridge until the four thirty mail train screamed past.

The movements were consistent. The signals perfectly executed. The metronome like rhythm of the railway system allowed little or no deviation. Wath was satisfied he knew the routine. His idea fitted.

There was just one problem. This meant going back to the old days, to being the man he no longer wanted to be. He sat for several hours staring into a fire. Memories flooded back, none of them good and every one of them something he wanted to forget. There was no other way. Every business man he knew had crossed the line at least once, done something illegal. Well, this would be it he decided, the last time he crossed the line. The only people who would pay would be the Government and they had taken enough from him it was time for them to give something back.

Satisfied, decision made, he started to plan.

Chapter Fifteen

Friday 19/3/1920

Wath had settled into a comfortable habit of going for a pint with Jimmy after he finished work on Friday and tonight was no exception.

In the Nelson the atmosphere was almost back to normal. Betty had been less than friendly after the Brass Band disaster but was slowly thawing. The domino team found it hilarious and were continually winding both parties up.

Jimmy bought the first round and was at last looking back to his old self. His face had the ruddy sheen Wath was used to not the ghastly slimy pallor of the previous weeks. Jack and Walt came to sit at the table alongside and joined Jimmy in a robust discussion of the potential strike situation. This was now the topic dominating conversation as the pandemic withered away. It appeared to Jimmy, who was a lot more informed than the rest of them, that a lot of the miner's bravado depended upon the Tri Partite Agreement with the dockers and the railway. If that solidarity wasn't there then everybody was in trouble. Wath sat listening half-heartedly, totally uninterested in the squabbles of miners, his thoughts constantly drifting to lorries and loans, while trying to find a way to smile at Betty but she was still stubbornly playing hard to get.

Around nine o clock with the pub at its busiest the doors swung open and a large balding man swaggered in. It was the man from the cement company. Three well-muscled men walked in behind him. Jack who was sat the side of Wath said out of the corner of his mouth 'That's George Mallinder, Henry's brother.'

Wath looked him up and down seeing the resemblance. Facially there was a likeness but George was a crude version of Henry, there was no attempt at sophistication, no subtlety about him at all. Apart

94

from a shirt and tie as a symbol of authority he was dressed like a worker, posing like a thug and achieving neither. He was big, fat and obnoxious, his ruddy face was already sweating and the slight stagger as he marched in hinted at him needing to find courage inside a glass before entering. Leaning on the bar he sneered across at Wath.

'You spending your ill-gotten gains pick pocket!' he called across the room, the hint of a slur in his voice. Everyone went quiet. The dominoes stopped, Betty looked across, a worried expression on her face, Jimmy straightened up at his side. Wath simply stared.

'I've got a message for you, coward, you stay away from my brother's family, do you hear. Otherwise, you'll regret it, unless you run away again, coward.' George turned slightly looking at Betty. 'Hope he's paying for his drinks love, not got a slate, cos he's not got a job any more have you pick pocket?'

Wath sighed, he thought this was over 'What do you want?'

'I want you to stay away from my brother's family.'

'And if I don't?'

'Well, then the boys here'll be having a word with you, persuade you otherwise.'

'Where's the Scot?'

'Couldn't make it this time.'

'Shame,' Wath stood up facing the three men. 'You done this before?'

The nearest man snarled 'More than once.'

They were the three men from before. This time they had jackets on which hid the tattoos but they were all well-muscled and none of them stank of drink, unlike George.

'Let's do it then, after you gents.' He pointed at George. 'You stay here.' He turned to Jimmy and pointing at George once more said 'Cover my back Jimmy, don't let him get behind me.'

Holding the door open he watched closely as the three men walked through. They did not appear to be carrying anything, their hands were empty, but they had workmen's boots on which probably had metal toecaps.

As Jimmy reached his side Wath said in a voice loud enough for everyone in the room to hear 'These three have done it before. They'll know when to stop. Keep him here. He'd be bloody nasty.'

The calm front he was presenting was a lie, it was one thing to talk about taking a beating, it was another thing to accept it. Internally Wath was speeding up, the external world was starting to decelerate, the movements of the three men heading towards the outside were in slow time as muscle memory flooded back. He flexed his shoulders, took long deep breaths and slowed his heart rate.

He looked at the doors in front of him, preparing himself to step through them. Images of barn doors flashed before his eyes, his nerves started tingling and his senses magnified. He stepped through the frosted internal door into the large entrance porch and let the door fall behind him.

As he did the barriers fell away and he was the man he used to be. The man walking into the barn, survival the only thing on his mind, death in his hands.

Stepping out into the street the three men split, one left, one right and one in the centre. Wath followed their movements closely, the one to his left appeared right-handed and was rocking on the balls of his feet. The one in the centre was flat footed resting on his heels. The one on the right was clenching and unclenching his fists. The man on the left needed stopping first then the one on the right, he could take his time with the one in the middle.

Moving into the entrance porch Wath heard the frosted internal door swing closed behind him shutting off the view from inside the pub. He strode out towards the three men. As he reached the front door he stretched up and, taking a deep breath, realising this was the point of no return, his promise gone, he grabbed for the pick axe handle hidden above.

His hand was closing on the handle when suddenly there was an uproar, the three men glanced up the street seeking the source of the commotion as Lucy came sprinting around the corner. She raced into the middle of the men screaming 'stop!' He let go of the handle as, ignoring the men, she bundled past, pushing Wath firmly in the chest, shoving him back into the pub. Reversing past Jimmy into the middle of the room he watched mesmerised as she turned from him and faced George.

'What the hell do you think you are doing?' she shrieked, flying into his face 'you have no right to do this, you keep out of my life. Do you hear?'

George threw his arms up 'He's got it coming to him, he has.'

Lucy was uncontrollable, a whirling dervish on a mission, she grabbed George by his tie thrusting it backwards, past his shoulder, pulling it tight around his neck. 'Not because of me!' she yelled into his face. Gasping George raised his hands to pull the tie down and as he leant back Lucy moved into him and kneed him as hard as she could in between the legs.

George grunted and fell forward his hands moving to his groin. Without stopping Lucy yanked his tie and pulled him towards the door, pushing it open with one hand, dragging him through the porch with the other. The three men outside looked at her in amazement as George stumbled to his knees in front of them. Standing behind George she pointed at them, 'If you three still want jobs in the morning, get him out of here and do not come back. Do you understand.' Then she stormed back inside.

Wath was open mouthed, rooted to the spot, every eye in the pub was on Lucy. She moved in front of him, breathing heavily, sweat drenched hair falling across her face, her hands on her hips. 'Well,' she said as calmly as her lungs would allow her to speak 'are you going to get the beers in or are you going to stand there looking useless all night long?'

Wath stuttered, looking first at Betty then at Lucy as she walked past him and sat at his table, 'Two beers Betty please, no make that

97

three, get Jimmy one.' He faltered still unable to absorb the scene in front of him. Shaking his head to clear his thoughts he sat alongside Lucy, Jimmy joined them from the door. Jack and Walt could not stop gawping at Lucy.

'You alright lass?' Jimmy asked, when she nodded, he smiled 'remind me never to fall out with you.' He burst into laughter 'That's the best thing I seen in years.'

Wath watched Lucy still sucking air as fast as she could, her hands were shaking, there was the slightest tremble on her chin. Fury still exploding from her eyes.

Betty placed three beers on the table and the noise of dominoes being shuffled returned. Lucy gave a long sigh then drank deeply from her pint. Looking at Wath she said

'Henry don't want you to see Alice, he thinks you'll be a bad influence. We had a row about it, last night.'

'Henry doesn't rule me.'

'I know. I know you won't give in. You're her father, you should get to see her. But I don't know what to do.'

'How did you know they were coming tonight.'

'Mac, the big scot. He didn't want anything to do with it, said he was lied to the first time. He left the concrete company today after words with Henry, told him he wasn't a fist for hire. Came to see me just now, told me what was happening. Henry sent George so he could claim he didn't know about it.'

Wath nodded. 'So, what do I do now?'

'Don't know.' Lucy passed her Marlborough's around. 'I tried Wath, I really tried.'

Chapter Sixteen

Saturday 20/3/1920

The following afternoon Wath sat in the signal box having a mug of tea with Frank.

'Jimmy told me about the fracas last night, do you think they'll try again.'

'Not sure, but you should've seen Lucy. She were bloody magnificent!'

'Thought you were chatting up that young barmaid? According to Jimmy she's all over you.'

'Jimmy talks too much.'

Frank laughed 'If he didn't tell me half of Nash Row would have. You're the best entertainment they've had in years. Lord Nelson's never been so busy.'

'You're taking the piss now.'

'Wish I was. Anyway, what're you going to do about work?'

'Don't know yet, not much around.'

'Got a bit of news. Joe Whiteley's decided to pack in carting. He can't do it all at his age and Jewel's already rejected two more blokes since you left.'

Wath looked up quickly and glared at Frank. 'If you make any comments about me and female horses we'll fall out.'

'Never entered mi head, but now you mention it you do—'

'Stop it, Frank!'

'Alright, calm down, it's only a bit of fun. Jimmy found it funny anyway.'

'What! You've not told Jimmy. Oh, for Christ's sake it'll be all over the Nelson by now.'

It was and the ribbing was continuous until the domino team ran out of horse, filly and mare puns, even Betty joined in with a neigh or two but eventually it calmed down. Wath cursed Jimmy every time a comment was made, unfortunately Jimmy found this immensely entertaining and spent half the night laughing at Wath.

When things quietened Jimmy got back on his soap box and started on about the pending miner's strike. He was convinced it would cause trouble with the railway unions. Once again Wath sat pretending to listen but really thinking about Joe packing in carting, there was an opportunity there if he only knew how to exploit it. As he mused Bill leant across from the domino table 'That's her lad, she was the one asking about yer.'

Wath looked across the pub, a stunning looking woman was at the bar with a man. Both appeared to be strangers, he was sure he had never seen her before. If he had, he would remember because she would stand out in any crowd. She was wearing a distinctive long-woven trench coat with patterned stitching on the arms, it had large lapels and a matching collar which was all fluffed up around a bright red silk scarf. On her head she wore a beret matching the chocolate brown of her coat. Her hair was pulled back in a bun underneath the beret and showed flashes of grey.

Gracefully confident she ordered a large whiskey while the man opted for a pint of bitter, they looked around and she noticed Wath looking at her. Picking up her whiskey she spoke to the man and they both moved to the far side of the room where she placed her drink on the table closest to the wall and he sat at the table alongside.

Assured their seats were secure she walked across the room, at her every step the room grew quieter until there was silence as she stood in front of Wath unashamedly looking him up and down, appraising him. He did the same to her.

There was something eerily familiar about her. The way she stood, the way she examined him, the expression on her face. A firm chin sat underneath a full mouth and strong cheek bones. Her nose was neither large nor small but straight. Smile lines at the side of her mouth showed the first signs of aging and matched the delicate crow's feet around her eyes. The eyes were bright and intense, shining with a keen intelligence and passionate inquisitiveness as she considered him.

Seemingly satisfied with her survey the woman said 'I'd like a chat if you don't mind.'

Wath pointed to the seat at the side of him.

'In private' she inclined her head 'be grand over there.'

'I'm comfortable here.'

'You don't know me, do you?'

'Give me a clue.'

Placing her hand on his knee, the woman leant forward and whispered into his ear. 'My name's Coleen does that help ye?'

She stood up straight, gave him a huge smile, tipped her head in the direction of her drink then walked back to her table. The dominoes were silent with Bill and Syd following her every move as she swayed through the room. Betty, Jimmy, Walt and Jack were all focused on Wath. Since the woman whispered into his ear, he had not moved a muscle, a look of shock frozen on his face.

The woman reached her seat, picked up her drink then looked Wath in the eye and tipped her head in the direction of the seat opposite once again. This time Wath picked up his pint and crossed the room, taking the seat she indicated. A subdued hubbub started as the locals returned to their drinks but they all cast a glance at the end table every ten seconds or so.

For a full minute they sat looking at each other before Wath said 'Thought you wanted to talk.'

'I do, but I've got to confess, I'm enjoying looking at you. Pretty boy ain't you.'

'What do you want Coleen?'

'I want to get to know you.'

'Why?'

'It's been a long time since I last saw you, a lot has happened, you're bigger than last time, much bigger.'

101

Wath's stare hardened, she was enjoying this. There was a glint in her eye and a smile playing around her lips but for Wath this was absurd, was she really saying she was the legendary Coleen.

'Are you telling me the stories are true?'

She motioned to the man at her side, 'Get the drinks in Patrick please.' As he moved to the bar she leaned forward 'I left you on that grave and I think you deserve an explanation, but before we go any further, I know about the problem with your daughter and I think I can help. And, just like you want to know her, I want to know you.'

She sat back and they both stared at each other. Wath felt his heart pumping, his nerves jumping. This woman in front of him was claiming to be his mother, a woman he had only heard stories about and then only as a myth. All his life he had believed the story was a hoax to disguise some young unknown unmarried mother's agony as she hid her pregnancy and gave her child away.

Now, here was Coleen saying that the rumours were true and, he could not deny it, as soon as she told him her name, he realised why she appeared familiar, there was a look to her eye, a set to her jaw and a swagger in her stance that he recognised. He saw it every time he looked into a mirror or passed a shop window, there was no doubt in his mind that they looked alike.

Suddenly his over worked brain made the connection – did that mean he was the son of a murderer? His stare intensified as his eyes narrowed. He could see she knew where he was in his thinking. She had been waiting for him to get to this point, to work it out himself.

'You need to talk.'

She nodded 'We both need to talk.'

Wath motioned to the man at the bar. 'What's with him, Patrick?'

'He's my minder. It's not safe for an Irish woman to be on her own over here, especially one with my surname, so he's here to look after me.'

Wath studied the man at the bar. There was a set to him which said he knew how to handle himself and an alertness which denied his attempt at being casual. Wath returned his attention to Coleen.

'Talk to me Coleen.'

She bowed her head, ready.

'This won't be easy and I need to go back a long way back to tell you the full story but your father Edwin inherited West Field Farm from Abel. We met at a dance, my parents were over here looking for work. After I married Edwin, they gave up and went back to Dublin. Everything was fine, the farm was never going to make us rich but it was a good healthy living. Then Hallett's brickworks discovered fireclay in the field next to ours and they started to badger us for access to our fields. Edwin refused point blank, wouldn't talk with them. It was his inheritance. They threatened him, abused me on the street, whipping up anti Irish feeling. That just made Edwin more determined than ever to refuse them. God, I never met a more stubborn man in my life.'

Patrick came back with the drinks and she motioned for him to return to the bar where he stood holding his pint, splitting his attention between Betty's figure and the two of them sat at the table.

'We lost a bull that year and Edwin blamed Hallett's. But by now there were four o them in partnership trying to buy him out. Hallett's the brickworks owner, Quade's the builders, Stanley's the Soap and Oil man and Henry Mallinder. They walked our land without permission and tested it and knew what was there. The fireclay was perfect for the glassworks and coke ovens and Hallett's wanted to make kiln liners. So, they pestered and made life as awkward as possible. They kept up the abuse, the threats. Edwin complained but no one did anything. The police were useless, probably being paid by the partnership.'

Patrick stood clear of the bar as Jimmy walked across 'You alright lad, want a pint?'

Wath pointed to his half-finished pint and the fresh one by its side. 'No, I'm fine thanks, catch you later.'

Jimmy nodded and motioned to Betty as Patrick resumed his position at the bar. Once he had settled down Coleen continued.

'Then one day, when Edwin was out in the fields, I was three months pregnant... with you. They turned up at the farm, all four o them, started pushing and shoving me and making all kind o threats. To be fair to Henry he refused to take part, said he drew the line at mistreating pregnant women and walked out.

'I reacted to their threats and their shoving and started hitting out and screaming and one o them pushed me to the floor. As I tried to get up, they kicked me, in the stomach, they laughed "Irish bitch" and kept taking turns kicking. I passed blood for a week - thought I'd lost you. Anyway, Edwin heard the commotion, came racing in and went berserk, you know the rest without needing the details. After they arrested him, I went to Manchester and stayed with cousins.'

Coleen took a packet of cigarettes out and passed him one. Wath picked up the distinctive mustard yellow packet 'Sweet Afton'. 'Perhaps you ought to change these if you don't want to stand out as Irish.' She tipped her head in acknowledgment,

'Habit' then blew blue smoke up into the ceiling and continued.

'I don't know how, but Henry found me and made me an offer for the farm. Two hundred and fifty pounds a year rent for the next twenty-five years. He was only young, the junior partner in the deal, the one going to work the extraction, wasn't owning the money to buy the farm outright. I just wanted a way back to Dublin so I agreed. Edwin was gone, I couldn't run it. Henry had the paperwork drawn up and I came back for the last time, to sign. I went inside and the shock o seeing it all, they hadn't cleaned it or anything, pushed me into labour and I birthed you.' She took a long pull on her cigarette and a sip of her whiskey. 'I was certain you'd be damaged after they kicked me and I couldn't bear the thought o going back a murderer's widow with a crippled child. To be completely honest I never expected you to live. So, I left you on the grave and went.'

She stared him straight in the eye as she said it. She had left him to die.

'Why on the grave?'

'Not sure. Some vague notion that someone might understand. But my head was in tatters, I wasn't thinking straight.'

She was toying with her glass spinning it around on the table.

'So why are you here?'

'I'm here to sell the farm to Henry, let him keep it. He can afford it now. My husband passed away and I need funds to support my family back in Dublin. I thought I could help you by making it a condition o the sale that you and I get to see the girl, Alice. After all she is my granddaughter.'

Wath stared at her. Sometimes help came from the strangest of places but Dublin was the last place he would have predicted.

'Thank you. I'd appreciate that.'

'So, what's your story pretty boy?'

They sat talking for a long time until Patrick came across 'We gotta go Coleen, the tram.'

Wath walked with them to the tram stop.

'What happens now?'

'We're staying at the Ferryboat Inn. Tomorrow I meet with Henry and his Solicitor and agree the details. After, I'll come to the pub and let you know what he said. Then me and Patrick go to London for three or four weeks. When we come back from there everything should be ready, I sign, Henry pays and I go back to Dublin.'

Wath walked back to Treacle Town happier than he had been in a long time. For the first time ever, it seemed a little bit of luck had blown his way. Truc it had come on a chill wind, a wind which had revealed dark rumours as being true, but that was irrelevant, there was now a chance he would get to see Alice.

Walking home he could see Fred in the signal box and he waved as he crossed the crossing. His mind was racing and he knew he would not sleep but Fred was never as friendly as Frank so he returned home and put the kettle on.

So, he was a Dyson – the son of a murderer. He sighed wondering if that was why he was such a good soldier. Was he born to kill. A stupid notion he realised but one which would not go away. He hated army life, the discipline, the orders, but put him in the trenches and he came into his own. Not anymore. He was past that. He repeated his oath to himself he was no longer that man, he was not going back.

He was confused by Coleen. She seemed good company but there was a hardness underneath the attractive exterior. She made no bones about it, did not try to disguise it. She had left him to die. That was a hard woman. A woman who could leave her child to die or, he realised, a desperate one and after witnessing her husband kill three men, she must have been desperate.

Stoking the fire, he recapped the evening. Lots had happened, then several thoughts collided and became one. Joe Whiteley was giving up his carting, he had a contract with Henry, could Coleen persuade Henry to transfer the contract to him? If she could then, using this he could get a loan from the bank and buy a lorry.

She was clear she had leverage on Henry, would she use her influence for him?

Again.

It was a long time before he fell asleep and he was awake with the five thirty Darfield Main house coal service to Immingham. The trams started at six so jumping on the first one he made his way to the Ferryboat Inn. He sat waiting outside, smoking. Sometime after seven thirty Patrick took a walk around the building and Wath approached him. 'I need a quick word with Coleen before you go '

Patrick looked him up and down, a look of pure contempt on his face. 'Wait here.'

Ten minutes later Coleen stepped out, confused. 'What's wrong?'

'Nothing but I want to ask you a favour.'

She raised an eye brow.

'Will you ask Henry to transfer Joe Whiteley's haulage contract to me.' He explained how Joe was finishing and how he needed a contract to fund buying a lorry.

'You want a contract with Henry despite him twice sending men to turn you over?'

'Aye.'

'You're mad.'

'Maybe, but it's the only way I'll get a lorry and there's no work anywhere.'

Coleen studied him, trying to decide whether or not to make the effort. There was calculation in her expression as she answered.

'Okay, I'll try. But the favours are stacking up pretty boy.'

'I appreciate that. Thank you.'

Wath was too excited to catch a tram or bus, he needed to burn some energy, so he set off walking back with his thoughts racing. He needed to see Joe. Henry was bound to try to fleece him over the contract details. Taking the route past the newsagents, which was the only shop open, he paid a ridiculous price for a few ancient apples but he needed to be sure he had an ample supply ready for when he arrived at Orchard Place. Jewel was in the field while Joe was sat in his kitchen in the house across the road.

He shouted and both Joe and Jewel were pleased to see him, she seemed to have no problems with old apples. Joe gave him a copy of the contract without hesitation. 'I'll keep going until the end of the month then you take over… if Henry agrees. If not, I'm contracted until the end of next year and I'm not sure I can manage that. But Henry don't like you, I'm not sure he'll agree.'

'Neither am I, but I've got to try.'

Despite trying as hard as he might, he could not stop himself from going to the Lord Nelson early. Deliberately sitting at the same table as the previous evening he nursed a pint waiting for Coleen. The regulars came in and all acknowledged him, taking their usual tables at the far end of the bar. After an hour of waiting Coleen and Patrick arrived. Jumping up Wath bought them drinks then sat down almost shaking with excitement.

Taking a sip of her whiskey Coleen passed cigarettes around, Park Drive, Wath noticed. Once they were settled, she finally looked at him and smiled.

'You owe me.'

'And?'

'Henrys agreed to transfer the contract on the condition you got a lorry a week before Joe packs in. You've got to go see him at his concrete place tomorrow. He's also agreed to us both seeing Alice when I come up to sign and after that you can see her every other Saturday.'

Wath shook his head in amazement. 'Jesus Coleen you must have some hold on him.'

'Oh, I can be very persuasive when I want.'

'I can't thank you enough.'

'Well, you can start by keeping me and Patrick in drinks tonight and talking some more about your past. I want to know how a pretty boy like you came to get them scars and still manage to look pretty.'

Chapter Seventeen

Monday 22/3/1920

The next morning Wath dressed in his new suit and walked to the concrete company on Mexborough Road.

The unit was as before, tidy. There was an air of controlled confidence about the place. An atmosphere which only comes when a business is covered in money, when the little things that disappear when money is tight were being done.

He walked into the yard and stood in front of the door to what appeared to be the offices and waited. George came out and three familiar faces emerged from the warehouse, standing watching him. There was sheer hatred in George's eyes as he growled at Wath. 'We aren't done. I'm having you.'

Wath ignored him. A few seconds later Henry appeared at the door and waved a hand. 'Leave it George,' then looking at Wath 'Follow me.'

Inside the building they went into what was obviously Henry's private office. It was at the end of a photograph lined corridor ending in a heavy wooden door. The two-inch thick door swung easily on well-greased hinges. Inside the office oak panels covered the walls while an oak desk which could have seated several families dominated the room. There was a powerful smell of wood polish and the perfume of wealth and authority.

Henry sat behind the desk in a leather chair and gestured for Wath to sit opposite him. He glared at Wath for a long time until he realised that Wath wasn't bothered by his frowning. He started to talk making certain by his tone that Wath knew who was in charge.

'How're you going to meet the contract?'

'I'm going to buy a lorry.'

'How?'

'Get a loan.'

'No lorry no contract.'

'Okay.'

'Let's discuss the terms.'

'No, the agreement was I am to take over Joe's contract, there's no terms to discuss, they're already agreed.' Wath pulled Joe's copy of the contract from his pocket.

'You shouldn't be seeing that.'

'You shouldn't be trying to change it.'

They stared at each other.

Neither man wanted to break the stare but both knew they were acting like schoolkids in the playground. There was business to be done and as usual with Henry money spoke louder than pleasure. Wath on the other hand had never had enough money to make the choice.

After a few seconds Henry got up and pulled a sheaf of papers from a cupboard. He threw them on the desk. 'That's two copies, sign them and I will, but there's a clause added in there that says if you fail to start on time I can cancel.'

Wath nodded and picked up the documents, taking his time he read them through. With the exception of the termination clause the unnamed contracts were the same as Joe's. Henry had them ready prepared, he must have been aware of Joe's decision to quit. Writing his name at the top of each document as party to the agreement Wath signed them and passed them back to Henry. With a scowl on his face Henry signed both and passed one copy to Wath.

As Wath rose to leave Henry said 'You don't know what you're doing do you?'

Wath looked at him quizzically.

'You've just got into bed with the devil.'

'I've dealt with worse than you Henry.'

Henry burst out laughing. 'Not me you stupid pillock. Coleen. You owe her now and she'll make you pay. I really could not have

110

wished for it to happen any better.' He was still laughing as Wath walked out of the door.

Jumping on the train at Mexborough Station Wath got off in Doncaster and walked to the Racecourse Garage. Inside were three gleaming Leyland lorries. Approaching the salesman, he asked about buying one. After a brief chat they went for a test drive around the race course paddock and he was shown the workings of the automobile.

It wasn't long before Wath was back inside the office showing him the delivery contract and explaining that he was going to the bank to arrange a loan but needed to have the vehicle details and an assurance that one was available. With a recession and the threat of a general strike sales were slow so, despite not having a deposit, the salesman agreed to provide the paperwork showing Wath could collect a four-tonne carrying capacity Leyland P in four weeks time. Fully armed with the paperwork Wath hurried back to the bank in Mexborough.

Pushing his way inside he found the manager he had spoken to previously and showed him the paperwork. Beaming delightedly the manager sat down with him, reviewed the details then asked Wath for proof of where he lived and where he would be keeping the vehicle.

'Surely you have a rent book? You can't just live somewhere for free.'

'No, I have an agreement where I don't pay rent.'

'I'm sorry but that is just not possible. Where do you live?'

'Treacle Town.'

The manager looked aghast. 'I'm sorry Mr Dyson but I cannot agree to a loan without both security and proof of residency. I'm afraid I must decline.'

Undeterred Wath tried three other banks. Each time becoming more desperate but all refused him credit.

His plans were falling apart.

111

It was a heavy walk back to Treacle Town. He had placed so much hope on getting a loan. He had been so confident that the rejection was deflating, he felt empty, worthless, the man from nowhere going nowhere. He was so engrossed in his misery he did not notice where he was walking until he reached the canal. He looked down at the water remembering the old days. Life in a boat, hard, transient, hated. He sat at the side of the lock.

What did he want from life? To be accepted, he had been an outcast all his life. Barges, Treacle Town, a non-commissioned officer. Not part of the ranks any more but not accepted by the lah ti dars.

But above that he wanted Lucy and Alice and the chance of that was being taken from him by pompous bank managers, another set of lah ti dars, who probably drank their tea from cups with their little finger extended into the air.

He started walking again his resolve hardening with every step. He would get a lorry. He would be accepted. He would get Lucy and Alice back. There was a way. There was always a way. It just needed him to step outside the system one last time. But every single business man he knew had stepped outside the system at least once. Faint sun glistened on the water in the canal, ripples carried dark and light to the side as the wind ruffled the surface of the water. Once more, that was all he needed, one more jump into the past, a last dip into the man he used to be. Then he could forget and become the man, the person, the father he yearned to be.

That evening Wath left the house at two am and walked up the tracks towards Wath Central Station. On the approach to the station a siding led off to the left and ended with a brick building with wooden doors over the track. It was the engineers trolley shed where they garaged their engineering trolley. After taking a quick check around Wath slid onto his back and squirmed under the door by the side of the track. It was a tighter fit than when he had explored here as a child but he was still able to get inside.

Lighting a match, he looked around the inside of the building, apart from the trolley there was nothing else inside, anything of value would be locked up in the engineer's workshop by the side of the station. He quickly inspected the trolley. It was a Sheffield Handcar with two handles linked to the wheels. By pumping the handle, the wheels turned and two men could easily manage fifteen miles an hour on a flat track. The brake was on but the engineers had still placed a wedge under both front wheels. Caution overkill. As he expected the trolley was well maintained, engineers were not going to put in excessive effort when grease and oil made the job easy.

Leaving the trolley, he took the match to the door and examined the lock. It was a metal rim lock screwed to the back of the wooden door. The cast iron keep where the latch sat when the door was locked was screwed to the door frame. It was held to the wooden frame by two metal screws and was probably the same one he had seen in his youth.

Satisfied he squirmed back under the door, walked across the tracks then crossed the road and followed the canal to Townend. Here he crossed the canal and road taking the path behind the George and Dragon and entered the stables in Orchard Place. Jewel was surprised to see him but he had an apple ready and she soon settled down. At the back of the stable Wath took a gallon can of the molasses which was used to supplement the horse feed and an old disused pump sprayer used to spray the horses with flea spray. He headed back, walking normally but still keeping to the shadows even though no one was around, twenty minutes later he was home, unseen.

Placing the items in the front room he curled up in his chair and slept.

His plan was starting to take shape.

Chapter Eighteen

Tuesday 23/3/1920

He was late up the next morning but still caught the ten-o clock train to Doncaster and by half past was inside Winfield's Pawn Brokers once again. The surly young girl simply looked at him without greeting and he asked to see Winfield. After a few seconds Winfield emerged from behind the door and stood looking at him quizzically.

'Yes?'

'I'd like a word in private please.'

'Wendy, if you would give us two minutes, please.' Winfield waited until the girl left the room and closed the door then asked 'well?'

'I'd like you to give me the paperwork for a loan for eight hundred pounds.'

'What! A loan for eight hundred pounds, are you mad?'

'No. Listen to me, I don't want a loan I just want the paperwork. Not the money, that'll come, I just want paperwork to back it up.' Wath focused his stare on Winfield, a direct intense stare which pinned Winfield. 'Here's what I propose. You give me the paperwork as if you have loaned me eight hundred pounds. Now if I borrowed that from the Bank, I would pay five percent interest or eighty pounds in total over two years. So, I will pay you eighty pounds in payments split evenly every month for two years in exchange for the paperwork.'

Winfield was shuffling under the glare of Wath's eyes. 'Let me get this right, you don't want any money and you will pay me eighty pounds over two years just for the paperwork as if I had lent you the money.

'That's it.'

114

Winfield did some quick calculations. 'That's three pounds six shillings and eight pence a month.'

'That's right. I will need a receipt every month to show that I have paid you the amount agreed in the paperwork including any interest. At the end of two years, it will say I have paid you back and the deal is over.'

'And that's all I have to do?'

'That's right but if the Police come you have to tell them you loaned me the money.'

'And will they come?'

'Probably.'

Winfield stared at him. Eighty pounds for a few of pieces of paper was very tempting and, even when he was a sallow youth dressed in second hand clothes, the man in front of him had always honoured their agreements in the past. He had something planned, something illegal which would generate eight hundred pounds.

But Winfield recalled their previous dealings when he had taken stolen goods from a half-starved boy and how he had read in the papers that the youth chose nine lashes of the birch rather than reveal who he had sold them to. There was a bond he could not define and then the medals. He now knew the medals were real. Winfield knew for a certainty that Wath had earned them. After his research into how they were won he was so impressed he had kept them.

Yes, he wanted to continue dealing with this strange tight-lipped enigma and here was a golden opportunity to ensure contact for the next two years while making money at the same time.

'Ok. I'll do it but I want four pounds a month and ten pounds up front.'

'Can't do ten pounds up front. I'll agree four pounds a month but that's it.'

No. I want ten pounds up front. Listen if the police come, they will be suspicious unless they can see the money leave my bank account. You have the money—'

'Will have.'

'Ok will have. Give me the money and I will give you a cheque for the same amount. But we must also have a contract. That way the police will be satisfied.'

After haggling for a few minutes more Wath saw the sense in what Winfield was saying and they shook hands on the agreement. Winfield made out two copies of a contract after Wath agreed to make the first payment at the end of the month including a ten-pound bonus for the original paperwork and cheque, paid when the cheque was handed over.

Taking one copy of the contract with him, Wath went back to the train station via the vegetable market. Tucked away at the back of the market was a tiny stall run by an Indian family selling exotic foods and spices. Wath bought a dozen dried hot chillies, a bulb of garlic, a piece of ginger root and a lemon before returning to Treacle Town.

Once back he threw the ginger root and most of the garlic onto the fire then, as carefully as he could, he chopped the chillies into small pieces before grinding them into a fine powder. It was a slow process using the rounded end of a ball peen hammer and an old frying pan, but eventually he had a dust which he poured into one of his mother's jam jars. He filled the jar with vinegar, squeezed in the lemon juice and added finely diced garlic before placing it on a shelf down the cellar.

Chapter Nineteen

Friday 26/3/1920

Early Friday morning was spent watching the trains and signals once more. Then after catching up on some sleep, Wath bussed it into Sheffield. At the Army and Navy surplus store he bought a leather motorcycle helmet, goggles and a battery flashlight. It was the easiest part of his itinerary but the most traceable so the purchase needed to be made in a different area. In the market he bought a second-hand pair of oversized dark blue overalls and leather gloves.

Returning home, he spent the afternoon filtering his chilli vinegar through a cloth and, taking great care, stored the liquid in a sealable jar before he ambled to the signal box where Frank was on duty. Wath climbed the steps and sat having a drink with a satisfied smile on his lips.

'What's got you so happy? Not seen you for a couple of days.'

'Been busy Frank and life is finally on the up.'

'Go on then.'

'Well, Henry has agreed to let me see Alice and he's agreed to transfer me the haulage contract from Joe Whitely. So, I get to see Alice and I've got work.'

'How the hell did you manage that?'

'The woman who called to see me the other day—'

'The one Fred saw?'

'That's her. Well, she claims to be the woman who left me in the churchyard and she is selling Henry some land and she had a word with him.'

'Bloody hell. Some word.'

'Aye that's what I thought, but who cares. I've got everything I want.'

'I thought you thought that horses were a thing of the past.'

'I do. Not using horses gunna get a lorry.'

'Pssh. How you gunna get a lorry.'

'Got a loan. Cos Henry gave me the contract it means I've got work to pay off the loan and the lorry is what they call security so they let me have a loan and the lorry gets delivered in just over three weeks and I become a haulier the week after. Just got to keep the monthly payments up after that.'

Frank looked at him incredulous. 'That's fantastic lad. I can't tell you how happy I am.'

Wath felt himself colour up slightly. He wasn't used to praise and while it was nice it was embarrassing. Then there was the small issue of him misleading Frank. He could lie with the best of them but not to Frank. He was the one man he respected and looked up to.

'What do you think about her?' Frank asked 'the woman who says she left you.'

Grateful for the opportunity to change subject Wath replied 'Truthfully, not sure. Says her name is Coleen which fits the stories. She seems fine but she did leave me.'

'Aye. But stories are stories she could have heard them and just said she was Coleen.'

'No. She knew Henry before she left and she is still dealing with him now. She's Coleen alright.'

'Has she said anything about that night?'

'Bloody hell this is worse than sitting in a cell with Goulding.'

'Just interested, you know how boring it is in here on your own.'

'Peaceful.'

'Boring. Well did she say anything?'

'Oh, for Christ's sake… just she wanted to get away, back to Dublin, didn't want to be lumbered with a child Said she thought I was crippled and would die.'

'Hmmm, she sounds lovely.'

Leaving Frank, Wath walked up to the pub. He was troubled, uncomfortable at misleading Frank – he didn't have the loan – but it was important to test his story before he got to the pub and if Frank believed him then he would be able to convince the rest with ease.

Inside the pub the usual crew were in and the usual banter ensued. But it wasn't long before Bill leaned over. 'Come on then lad. Don't keep us in suspense who's the bonnie woman and where have yoU been the last few days? Betty's been beside herself in case you take up with someone twice your age.'

'I heard that Bill,' shouted Betty from the bar 'be careful how you answer him Wath. I'm listening.'

'It's nothing like that Bill. She claims to be the woman who left me in the churchyard as a baby. Wants to get to know me a bit and she wants to see Alice.'

'What she's Coleen Dyson?'

'Well Coleen something or another.'

'So, the stories are true?'

'Which ones?'

'That she came back and left the Devil's whelp as Edwin's revenge on Wath.'

'Bloody hell Bill. Hang on - the Devils whelp. I got enough problems with Goulding as it is. I don't need other people seeing me as a devil or revenge!'

'Well, you ant been sweetness and light up to yet, have you?'

'No. But that's still a bit strong and I'm doing my best to be right. You asked where I've been the last few days… well, I've got a haulage contract and a lorry being delivered so things are looking up not down.'

'A lorry! How'd you do that?'

'I got a delivery contract and used it to get a loan and used the loan to buy a lorry. It comes in three weeks' time. I'll give you all a free ride.'

Bill looked across at the bar. 'Get your hooks into this one lass, he's going places he is.'

'Aye' said Syd 'in a lorry and he's taking us all for a ride.'

119

Saturday 3/4/1920

It being Easter Wath excused himself from his Thursday night/Friday morning vigil and relaxed enjoying the reduced smoke and rail traffic. Saturday night he resumed his preparations. That night he walked down the track past the Adwick bridge on the Midland line and waited at the back of the concrete works until the four am sleeper passed. It was Easter weekend and no one would be at work until six o clock Tuesday but Wath still took his time and surveyed the compound ensuring it was empty. There was large fence around the works on the road side but with the steep embankment no one had bothered with a fence on the railway side. Sliding down the embankment he entered the works compound. Once inside Wath made his way to the storage bays and searched. First, he took a wheel barrow and dragged it up to the top of the embankment. Then he carried up a large tarpaulin and several ropes and using the wheel barrow transported them all back home on the path at the side of the track. Satisfied, the next day he spent some time cutting holes in the corners of the tarpaulin and threading rope through.

Sunday 4/4/1920

At two o clock the next morning he returned to Twentieth Century Concrete with the wheel barrow and once again surveyed the area for half an hour before moving. Using the wheel barrow, he took three bags of sand, a dozen house bricks and removed two of the metal pegs holding down a tarpaulin over a sand store before hiding them all behind the wall by Adwick bridge.

With some time to spare he took the pegs and hammered two into the ground above the bridge before returning the wheel barrow

120

to the cement compound. Picking up an old sweeping brush from the side of the warehouse he made his way back home.

He was almost ready.

Now all that was required was patience as he waited for word of his imminent lorry purchase to filter through and become old news.

Chapter Twenty

Thursday 8/4/1920

Finally, the night was here and Wath prepared himself, filling the pump with his chilli spray and putting all the items he needed out of sight behind the terrace. He left the house at around half past one in the morning. Marching down the tracks he slid under the trolley shed doors. Standing up he placed the dimmed flash light on the trolley pointing at the lock. Using his screw driver he removed the two screws holding the cast iron keep and placed it on the floor at the side of the door. Swinging the door open he removed the wedges and placed them on the trolley bed then climbed onto the trolley and, releasing the brake, began pumping the handle up and down which started the well-greased cogs turning enabling him to propel the trolley out of the shed.

Driving the trolley past the engineering sheds he moved quickly down the track until he approached the signal box. Fred was on tonight and he had a habit of dozing in the chair by the stove. Wath halted the trolley and, waiting until his eyes adjusted, made sure Fred was in his usual position. Immediately he saw this he moved past until he was on the far side of Treacle Town where he stopped again. Jumping off the trolley he ran around the back of the terrace and grabbed the tarpaulin, ropes and other pieces of kit from where he had left them. It was awkward getting the tarpaulin onto the trolley in a position enabling him to work the handles while keeping the pump upright but taking care he managed it.

Then came the long run pumping the handle up and down, maintaining speed as he followed the colliery curve to the northern junction with the MNER line. Here he jumped down and using the brake stick forced the points open and manoeuvred the trolley onto the fresh line. Jumping back on board he started pumping again and followed the mainline until he reached the bridge at Adwick crossing. Taking a few minutes to get his breath back he put on overalls and gloves and tied sacks around his feet before he started to unload his kit.

Firstly, he secured the six ropes to the trolley before letting them drop down from the bridge over the side of the embankment. Unfolding the tarpaulin across the railway lines he poured the molasses over it and using the sweeping brush spread it until the whole of one side of the tarpaulin was covered. It was awkward and he had to fold the tarpaulin several times, keeping it inside the rail track. This he decided was the worst thought out part of his plan. The tarpaulin needed to be heavy with one side sticky, the molasses was perfect but applying it was difficult and messy. He could not afford to get any of the molasses onto himself so it was a long slow job.

Finally finished he placed the empty can in a sack and threw the ruined brush to the side. Then he tied two corners of the molasses drenched tarpaulin to the pegs on top of the bridge slowly releasing the tarpaulin over the edge, molasses side out, lowering it using ropes tied to the bottom corners. Running down the embankment he checked the fit, apart from a one-foot gap at the bottom the entrance under the bridge was fully covered.

Ducking under the bridge he laid the house bricks in a row across the road some three feet behind the hanging tarpaulin. Then scrambling back up the embankment he slid two sleepers down its side before positioning them across the road some four feet away from the bricks with the three bags of sand packed as ballast behind them. The sacks on his feet made the going more difficult and the overalls left him soaked in sweat.

Running back up the embankment, now gasping for breath, he grabbed the two wedges, leather helmet, goggles, scarf and pump sprayer before sliding back down to the road side and finally sitting down, panting heavily. He checked his watch, ten to four. Relaxing as best he could his breathing started to return to normal as he put on the helmet, tied the scarf across his face, positioned the goggles on his forehead and waited.

Mentally he checked himself, making certain all the jobs had been completed, that everything was ready. Now it all depended upon timing. The pit lorry carrying the wages from the bank had driven under the bridge at between five past and ten past four for the past four Friday mornings. The driver and guard habitually left the bank in Mexborough at exactly four-o clock which gave them time to drive to Manvers Main Colliery and be ready for the wages clerks to count the money into individual pay packets allowing them to pay the night shift as they came out of the pit or left the coke ovens at six o clock.

At four o clock Wath heard the signal change for the overnight sleeper on the MNER line. This meant that the signals were in his favour until the Royal Mail service at half past four. He pulled the goggles over his eyes and checked the position of the wedges and the pump.

His heart started to thump.

He took long slow breaths concentrating on calming himself and being ready to move. All he could do now was wait and hope the normal routine was followed and the timings matched.

It seemed to take an age but eventually he became aware of the sound of a lorry in the distance coming closer. Pressing himself into the embankment he waited. A lorry came around the bend slowing as it approached the bridge.

It was the pit lorry.

The weak headlights picked out the tarpaulin hanging in front of the tunnel. Wath had a momentary panic as he wondered if the driver would see the shine of the molasses and realise the danger, but no - he came on.

In the instant before he hit the tarpaulin the driver sensed something was wrong. The impact of the lorry broke the weakened corners and the heavily weighted tarpaulin fell across the cab of the lorry, encasing the driver and his mate.

At the same moment the front wheels hit the house bricks laid across the road. The solid tyres thumped the bricks and the whole lorry jumped up into the air. The driver slammed the brakes on hard and the lorry screeched across the tarmac until it hit the sleepers behind the house bricks, crashing to a halt.

Wath only had seconds before the driver recovered, he raced from cover and rammed the wedges in front of and behind a back wheel. The lorry was immobilised. The driver and guard would be testing the doors and finding the sticky tarpaulin holding them in. They should be confused and disoriented, not sure what was stuck to the lorry, trapping them inside. The sweet sickly smell alien and inexplicable.

Jumping back to where he had been waiting, he grabbed the pump. Running to the passenger door he pumped the handle furiously and pushed the nozzle under the tarp spraying into the cab. He could hear the frantic cries of the driver and his passenger as the pepper spray filled the interior, the molasses weighted tarpaulin holding the spray inside. As the spray bit into their eyes the two men would be bewildered, trying to stop the pain, keeping their eyes closed, frantically seeking a way out but the tarpaulin trapped them.

He kept spraying for a full fifteen seconds then placed the pump at the side of the lorry and jumped up onto the back of the truck.

Using his knife, he sliced the canvas covering the boxes and grabbed the six ropes hanging from the bridge. He had been uncertain how many boxes there would be and it was too risky to observe them being loaded so he gambled on six as that was the number he had witnessed when the Thrybergh Bottom lorry emptied them at the bank. It was coincidentally also the most he could carry comfortably on the trolley.

Pulling the canvas back there were only two boxes so with six ropes he had seriously over compensated. He quickly tied ropes to the handles of both of the boxes listening to the screams and protests from the driver and his mate as they bundled around trying to get

125

out of the cab onto the road. Finishing tying off the boxes he jumped down and grabbed the pump once more.

Both men had now managed to fumble their way out of the cab, crying and rubbing their eyes furiously. They were covered in molasses from where they pushed the tarpaulin to escape the cab. One man was on his knees being sick in the road while the other was holding onto the side of the lorry shaking his head desperately.

Wath pumped the spray again then stopped. Spraying them again was probably unnecessary and malicious. The first spray would leave them virtually blind for thirty minutes or so and in discomfort for at least six possibly up to ten hours but there would be no lasting effects. If he sprayed them again there may be worse side effects. They were only doing their job and he wished them no lasting harm. He just needed them incapacitated for a few minutes more.

Satisfied they were out of action he rescued the wedges and scrambled back up the embankment. He threw the pump and wedges onto the trolley and started to heave the boxes from the bed of the wagon with the ropes. One at a time he pulled them off the lorry and over the wall placing them and the attached ropes onto the trolley.

He ripped the canvas sacks from his feet, the gloves from his hands and pulled the overalls off shoving them all into a canvas sack making sure he did not transfer any of the molasses they had collected onto his clothes underneath. Placing the sack on the trolley he checked himself again. He was fine. He threw the spare ropes onto the trolley.

Everything he left behind at the scene originated either from the side of the track or Twentieth Century Concrete.

Henry would have some explaining to do.

Starting to pump the trolley handles he could see the signals in the distance were still in his favour but even so he knew he had little time. The lorry had been slightly on the late side and his timings were now critical. If he did not get onto the colliery curve before the

126

four thirty Royal Mail service came down the track, he would be in for a head on collision with a mainline engine going at full speed.

Every muscle was screaming as he pumped, with the gradient against him he slogged down the track, gasping with the effort as he approached the junction and raced past it, the brakes screeched, sparks flying, as he hit them as hard as he could. Jumping off he removed the brake stick he had left earlier flinging it into the field at the side as the points sprang back.

Leaping back onto the trolley he kicked the reverse lever and pumped the handle as fast as he could. He was still going uphill, only slightly and not for long but the effort was excruciating.

Slowly the trolley started to move, easing its way along the track. He was only five yards past the points when the signal dropped and the points changed. It was now urgent the train was in sight flying down the rails towards him.

Pumping violently, his muscles cramping, he battled around the curve, desperate to get out of the way of the mainline engine. Forty yards later he relaxed as the engine flashed by, missing him by inches.

He leant against the pump handles and rested, sweat dropping off him. He still had much to do. Pumping frantically once again he raced to top speed as he made his way back through the colliery curve onto the GCR line and glided to a stop opposite Treacle Town.

Jimmy should be asleep in the back room but he still tiptoed as he lifted the boxes off the trolley and made his way across to the terrace. Staying track side, he made his way to the opposite end of the terrace from his house to the one vacated by the Jenkinson's and now boarded up.

Removing the coal cellar cover from the side of the front door and using the attached ropes he lowered the boxes into the cellar. Even as a child he could not fit through the cellar opening but the money boxes went through easily. He then dropped the pump, the sack containing the overalls, the goggles, and the helmet on top of them and replaced the cover.

Trotting back to the trolley he started pumping once again, he was so tired he was almost careless as to whether or not Fred saw him but he could see he was still hunkered down in his chair.

Parking the trolley back inside its shed, he replaced the wedges and the cast iron lock keep, screwing it tightly into place, then squirmed under the door before staggering back home.

Putting a kettle on he took off all his clothes inspecting them minutely for any molasses. There was a small stain on the right sleeve of his shirt from where he pushed his hand into the cab as he sprayed. He took it off and along with the scarf he threw it onto the fire.

Checking the time, just before five, he dressed in his normal clothes and taking his hurricane lantern, as the five-o clock service passed by, he made a noisy show of visiting the outside toilet after which he went into the hen run deliberately disturbing the hens as he gathered two eggs. Leaving the hen house, he saw Fred's shadow cross the darkened signal box as the signalman watched Wath's movements from inside.

Back in the kitchen he placed his boots in the sink with a solution of diluted bleach just covering the soles then wiped his face and hands carefully with a towel soaked in water containing baking powder. This was unnecessary as the goggles and scarf had done their job and stopped the pepper spray but it was a precaution in case of the worst.

He made sure his scarf and shirt were fully burnt on the fire then scrubbed his boots checking the soles were clean. He could not afford for a speck of molasses to be left.

It was now approaching five thirty so he fried bacon and eggs and ate slowly. At five to six as the sun started to filter through, he took a cup of tea outside and sat on the step rolling a cigarette. At exactly one minute to six-o clock Bill Deakin walked past the yard

128

heading to the signal box to relieve Fred. Noticing Wath sat outside Bill waved and shouted.

'Lovely day.'

'Aye.'

Waiting until Bill turned the corner Wath fell back inside, collapsed into the chair and was fast asleep within seconds.

Chapter Twenty One

Friday 9/4/1920

Following their established Friday night ritual Wath banged on Jimmy's door at six o clock.

'Hang on I'm not ready yet.' Jimmy yelled.

'Gunna have a chat with Frank. Give me a wave when you're ready.'

'Will do.'

Climbing the stairs Wath smiled at Frank, took his jacket off and accepted a mug of tea.

'My timing gets better'

'You're bloody predictable that's what you are. Jimmy'll be here in ten.' Said Frank pointing at a mug sat waiting by the tea pot. 'I've been thinking about Coleen.'

'Yeah.'

'Yeah. Have you read the paper?'

'Don't be daft.'

'Well, there's an article in the Times today on about Irish protests in London and they mention Coleen Collins giving a speech.'

'So?'

'Is that her? Your Coleen.'

'She didn't give me a surname.'

'If it is be careful, her husband was executed after the Easter Rising and their son is currently in Mountjoy prison for armed insurrection.'

'Said her husband passed away.'

'Did she mention her son?'

'No.'

'Watch yourself, if she's IRA, she's bloody dangerous. Hello, what have we here?'

Wath followed his gaze out of the window, PC Goulding was walking into the yard with an unknown man at his side. Together they watched as the pair approached Wath's house and knocked on the door.

'Looks like Goulding's found another reason to hassle me.'

'They told me in the Post Office that there's been a robbery.'

'Aye, I heard the same.'

'I heard it was the pit wages.'

'Whatever, looks like I'm the usual suspect.'

'You gunna be okay?'

'Aye. See you in a minute.' Wath left the signal box and walked up to the two men.

Goulding was stood barrel chested glowering at Wath. The other man was smaller and thinner, surveying Wath with a studious air.

'What's up?'

'Where were you last—'

'I'll handle this thanks Constable.' the unknown man cut in, stepping forward and taking an empty pipe from his lips before placing it in his pocket. 'Detective Smedley, I would like to ask some questions.'

Wath turned his stare from Goulding and looked at the man. Wath would have taken bets he was in the Masons. He was completely unassuming. A common place face, common place brown hair and a common place bland expression. A grey suit, white shirt and blue tie topped with a grey fedora with a matching blue band around the rim tried to give him status but came across as contrived. The pipe was an affection, another part of the image he was trying to project. But there was something in the eyes, something that gave a hint of natural cunning.

'Ask away.'

'Inside would be better.'

'I'm going out and would prefer to get this over with.'

'Ok. Where were you in the early hours of this morning?'

Wath pointed at the door 'In there, asleep. Why?'

131

'Can anyone verify that?'

'No. I live alone.'

'Wonder why' muttered Goulding.

Smedley glared at Goulding. 'There was a robbery this morning and PC Goulding believes you may have something to do with it.'

'PC Goulding thinks I have something to do with everything that happens around here.'

'That is as may be but you do have a reputation.'

'Had a reputation detective.'

Smedley frowned as if he was confused, a reputation was a reputation they did not go away. The expression contradicted the suit, the pipe, it was the eyes again. They gleamed insight, calculation, the rest was a sham. This man was an actor.

'Do you mind if we have a look around?'

'Be my guest.' Wath waved a hand at the door. Unconcerned. He too could act.

The two men pushed into the house and Wath sat on the step rolling a cigarette as Jimmy emerged.

'What's going off.'

'There's been a robbery and Goulding's blaming me as usual.'

'I heard, today at work. Some armed gang robbed the pit lorry carrying the wages this morning. Is he blaming you for that?'

'Don't know, he hasn't exactly said what he's blaming me for, just a robbery.'

After a while the two police officers came out of the house and looked at Jimmy as Wath stood up.

'And you are?' asked Smedley recovering his pipe.

'Jimmy Cotton and I live just there' he said nodding his head at his door. 'and I had nothing to do with robbing no wages.'

'We didn't mention no wages.' Said Goulding.

Smedley scowled at him again before appraising Jimmy's missing arm and the awkward ankle then said 'Thank you Mr Cotton but we are trying to verify where Mr Dyson was at around four thirty this morning.'

132

'I've told you I was in there asleep.'

'The beds do not appear to have been used Mr Dyson.'

'I don't sleep very well in a bed I sleep in the chair.'

Smedley looked at his highly polished boots, took in the scars and said 'Army? ... Trenches?'

Wath nodded 'Aye.' His tone implied sarcasm – as if the man was a raving genius managing to add two and two together but internally Wath knew the Detective was trying to put him at ease. Trying to get him sloppy.

'I understand.' He looked down at his own highly polished shoes 'It took me a while as well.'

There it was, they had a bond, a common history, a joint experience, they could be friends. Wath didn't give a fig about polished shoes.

'Reputation or not we will be watching you Mr Dyson - until we can establish where you were.' And there was the threat. I can be your friend – or not.

There was a clatter in the distance, a coke oven retort emptying. Even as they heard it Wath and Jimmy moved to the side placing their backs to the wind. Both of them held their breath as the putrid cloud ran down the track, engulfed them, then moved on.

Goulding and Smedley took the volley full frontal. Goulding had the sense to close his mouth and hold his breath but Smedley almost choked as he gagged on the sulphurous cloud.

'What was that?' he gasped at Wath.

'Progress detective. That's the taste of progress.'

Suddenly Jimmy burst in 'He was here at five o clock.'

'What?'

'Him. Wath. He was here at five o clock this morning.'

'How do you know?' spluttered Smedley wiping his face with a white handkerchief. He grimaced as he saw the black stain. His carefully constructed image was gone. Wath and Jimmy had grins on their faces while Goulding grappled with a satisfied smirk.

133

'He went to the toilet just as the five-o clock from Manvers came past.'

'You saw him.'

'Yeah, well I saw his lantern, reckon Fred must have seen him.'

'Fred?'

'Yeah, the signal man.' Jimmy pointed at the box.

'Ok we'll ask him.'

'You'll have to comeback cos he's gone now. That's his mate Frank. Fred'll be back at ten tonight.'

'Thank you, Mr Cotton, you've been exceptionally helpful. Mr Dyson.' Smedley nodded to Wath, blew his nose on the handkerchief, thrust his still unlit pipe into his pocket, glared at Goulding and marched away. Goulding trotted after him not bothering to hide his grin.

The Nelson was buzzing with the news of the robbery. Everyone had a different theory. Wath sat mesmerised as the armed gang theory gained the ascendency while the amount stolen rose until it hit the ten-thousand-pound mark.

Jimmy regaled the regulars with the story of Wath being accused by Goulding and how him and a Detective had searched the house, delighting his audience with the tale of the detective choking on the coke ovens smoke. Syd laughed 'So Wath what gun did you use and did you say "stick em up" like in the western books?'

'Nah, just hit em round the head with sand bags, did the trick perfect.' He sat back and listened as the Syd took up the commentary.

'It weren't anybody from round ere. It was foreigners.'

'Why do yer say that?' questioned Bill

'Cos it was Easter last weekend. Think of all the holiday pay. Anybody local would've known and done it then' Syd nodded sagely, confident in his analysis 'it were foreigners.'

'Frenchies?'

'Nah Cockneys. They ent got the brains they was born with.'

134

'They've got our wages.'

'It'll rattle the Unions you know' said Jimmy back on his favourite subject. 'men not getting paid on time.'

'They'll be insured.' Said Bill

'No way, it's the Government int it, they never bother with insurance they'll just pay it out of taxes.'

'If they don't get it back, looks as though they've brought people in, if that Detective were anything to go by.'

'Would you trust Goulding to sort it?'

'Only thing Goulding's good for is blaming Wath. But hey they've got Sherlock Holmes on the case now.'

'He's only good for murders.'

'What! Somebody was killed.'

'Told yer… it was Cockneys.'

Chapter Twenty Two

Monday 12/4/1920

The weekend passed without further incident though the rumours surrounding the robbery continued to grow. Wath waited until Jimmy was at work and at ten o clock on Monday morning as the Barnsley to Doncaster passenger service trundled past, he knocked on the signal box door. Fred was in attendance resetting the signals.

'Hi Fred, mind if I borrow the ladders, hen house roof needs attention.'

'Yeah, go ahead. By the way a Detective came round asking about you.'

'Aye seems Goulding's been in his ear.'

'Bloody menace that man, any road asked me if I'd seen you the morning of the robbery.'

'I was asleep and can't prove it.'

'Aye but yer went to the loo at five cos I saw yer. So, I told him.'

'Okay thanks Fred. Might shut him up but Goulding just wants me.'

'Like I say the man's a menace.'

Wath took the ladders from under the signal box and made a long pretence of repairing the hen house roof. Then he rested the ladders underneath his kitchen window and made lunch.

After Bill replaced Fred in the signal box Wath took the ladders inside and lifted the loft hatch. Using the ladders, he climbed into the loft taking a workman's snap bag, four grain sacks, a bag of tools and his flash light. Pulling the ladders up behind him he replaced the hatch cover then started across the attic.

The roof space in the terrace was where the original builders had saved cost. The internal walls of the terraces only reached the bedroom ceilings, apart from the chimneys which reached the roof everything in between was one large void. Taking care to step on the beams and not fall through the plaster it was just a stooped walk to traverse from one end of the terrace to the other.

Reaching the far terrace Wath lifted the hatch cover to the Jenkinson's and lowered the ladder. Climbing down there was enough light still coming through the boarded-up windows for him to make his way to the cellar without using the flash light.

As he passed the rooms, he recalled how they were when he last saw them. Tidy. Now there was a mess of clothes on the floor and drawers were pulled out, cupboard doors left open. Suggett had been through the house before boarding it up. Wath took this as a good sign, Suggett would not want anyone coming inside.

Once in the cellar he switched the flash light on. Pulling the metal boxes off the coal he placed the boxes carefully on the floor and waited until a train went past then, as it did, smashed the locks using a lump hammer and cold chisel. The passing of the train covered the noise. It needed two trains to pass before he had fully broken the locks but that was the noise all finished. Using the plier's, he bent the hasps back and opened the boxes.

The first was labelled Coke Ovens, inside paper money was neatly bound while coins were stacked in bags. There was a summary receipt in an envelope on top. Nine hundred and seventeen pounds, four shillings and six pence.

A smile crept across his lips.

The lorry was already paid for, the box for Manvers Main contained one thousand six hundred and eighty-four pounds eleven shillings and three pence a grand total of two thousand six hundred and one pounds fifteen shillings and eight pence.

He sat back against the wall amazed. All he could think was how unbelievable it was that the pit believed the transfer was safe simply because it was in a lorry.

Well, they wouldn't again.

He counted the notes and packed nine hundred and ten pounds comprising of one pound and ten-shilling notes into the workman's snap bag. It bulged with the volume. There were only forty of the large denomination five-pound notes and Wath was convinced the numbers would be recorded somewhere so he placed these in one of the envelopes and stuffed it under one of the empty boxes. The rest of the money he divided roughly between the four grain sacks then tied them up using the ropes before laying the ropes out.

Standing on the pile of coal and metal boxes he loosened the mortar in between the bricks underneath the coal cellar cover. Taking the poker from the back fire he rammed it into the gaps in the mortar, its metal rod spanning the coal hole chute and tied the ropes to it. The ropes were invisible under the cover but available from the outside when the cover was lifted, enabling him to pull the sacks containing the money out of the cellar without having to go through the process of climbing through the lofts.

Climbing back through the loft hatch, he pulled the ladders up and screwed the hatch cover to the cross beams. No one would be coming up that way without making a lot of noise.

Once back home he was twitchy. The whole process had taken less than an hour but this was the dangerous part. If Goulding or Smedley came, he would be caught red handed with nine hundred pounds on him. He returned the ladders then caught the train to Doncaster.

Within minutes he was inside the pawnbrokers asking for Winfield. Winfield left Wendy at the counter and gestured for Wath to follow him into the back room. Here he carefully counted the notes then passed across a cheque made out to the Lorry Salesroom for eight hundred pounds. The transaction completed Winfield looked at Wath.

'Can I ask a favour?'

Wath shrugged his shoulders.

'Will you walk to the bank with me please. This is rather a lot of money.'

Wath smiled. 'Aye.'

Together they walked to the bank where Winfield deposited the money and they parted with a handshake. Unable to stop himself constantly looking over his shoulder for any sign of Smedley Wath walked to the racecourse arriving at the salesroom at four o clock and gave the Salesman the cheque. Then he visited two banks and opened accounts in each with different amounts from the one hundred pounds he had left. Finally relaxing he made his way back to Treacle Town.

Keeping a low profile for the next few days Wath made a show of visiting potential customers for his soon to be started haulage company. Using the cover of seeking customers Wath also opened bank accounts at different banks in Mexborough and Barnsley. By the end of the week, he had safely deposited a further four hundred pounds across four accounts, the rest he left in Jenkinson's cellar.

That was enough for now. He had a business to run. He was comfortable that the sand contract would ensure the business was solvent but if it was to flourish, he needed more work. One man with a horse and cart could only do so much, however with a lorry he would be at least twice as efficient. But Wath wasn't satisfied with just making ends meet.

He would make this work and show Lucy.

Chapter Twenty Three

Monday 19/4/1920

On the Monday he caught the train to Doncaster and walked with unrestrained excitement to the Racecourse salesroom. His lorry was waiting, sparkling in the morning sun. The salesman gave him a tour and showed him all the service points, a few tips on driving and a long lesson on starting the engine. The starting handle kicked like a mule and if operated incorrectly it could inflict a broken wrist.

However, the biggest warning came regarding the brakes. Both the foot and hand brake connected to the rear axle and were prone to wear. The lorry could reach speeds of twenty miles an hour plus, but at that speed the brakes needed applying well before the designated stopping site because they were simply not powerful enough especially if it had a heavy load on board. He advised Wath not to go faster than the prescribed fourteen miles per hour and to check and maintain the brakes on a regular basis.

Wath decided he would be a lot slower than recommended until he felt comfortable.

After half an hour Wath set off. At first, he found the gears brutal and several grating crunches taught him how to use the clutch. Pulling onto the long stretch on the Doncaster to Barnsley Road he managed to find fourth gear. With no glass in the screen or doors, he felt the wind whipping against him as, despite his earlier promises, he moved up to full speed. Twenty miles an hour was faster than most could run for a sustained distance and the lorry was cruising. The effect was exhilarating.

At that speed the solid tyres bounced off any bump or pot hole and the leaf suspension barely compensated so Wath decided the salesman was right and his own early promise made sense, a sedate ten to twelve miles an hour was the optimum speed.

His first stop was Twentieth Century Concrete where he confirmed ownership of the lorry and agreed a starting date of the following Monday. Then he drove up to Orchard Place and showed Joe his new acquisition. Joe was delighted but Jewel was unimpressed as he forgot to bring apples. Confirming everything with Joe he returned to Treacle Town. After lunch he practised reversing and turning in the narrow yard under the watchful eye of Fred who was on duty in the signal box.

Tuesday 13/4/1920

At six o clock he picked Jimmy up and drove to the Lord Nelson where he gave the locals a ride before parking the lorry back in Treacle Town for the night. His mind was on fire and it was a long time before he fell asleep. Despite this he was up early and had nearly finished cleaning the lorry at eight o clock when Smedley and Goulding marched around the corner.

Smedley was raging, not bothered with niceties or subtleties he plunged straight in. 'Is that yours?'

Wath ignored him and continued to scrub the wheel he was working on.

'I said is that yours?'

'Answer him lad.' Boomed Goulding.

Wath stood up and faced him. 'It's mine and I'm about fed-up o you.'

Goulding puffed himself up and balled his fists. 'You can't afford that. You robbed the wages.'

Smedley held a hand up for Goulding to stop. 'Look at it from our point of view.' Wath could see he was trying to calm down. The effort at self-control was colossal. 'There's been a robbery and suddenly you buy a lorry.'

'I bought the lorry before the robbery. I did it with a loan.'

'Bullshit.'

'Wait there.'

Wath walked over to the door where his jacket was hanging from the door knob. From the inside pocket he pulled several sheets of paper and took them to Smedley.

'That's a contract for haulage services, that's an agreement to borrow eight hundred pounds and that's a contract to buy a lorry.'

Smedley took the documents and examined them.

'I'll have to verify these with the other parties.'

'Do what you want but them agreements are not leaving my side.'

'When did you do this?'

'Read the papers.'

Smedley took a long time looking through the papers.

'If I have this correct you agreed the haulage contract eighteen days before the robbery, the lorry purchase the same day and borrowed the money the day after.'

'Sounds right.'

'So, you are now in debt and in need of funds. A little robbery would help.'

'Don't be stupid Smedley. I've got PC Plod here breathing down my neck. I can't do a thing without being watched and nothing happens without me being accused. I got a loan. The contract means I can pay it back. Go ask Henry and the others but stop bothering me.'

'Oh, I will ask the others and just for the record, I don't believe a word you say.'

'Funny that cos I don't give a monkey's what you think.'

That evening he went for a drink in the Nelson and rather than sit at his usual table he sat at the bar talking to Betty. The two youngsters were in as were the domino team, the familiar click clack in the background. The frosted door swung open and, in what had become an automatic reaction, Wath turned to look.

142

Pc Goulding dressed in civilian clothes shouldered his way to the bar. There was nothing to stop him having a drink when off duty but this was the first time Wath had ever seen him in the Nelson. They stared at each other for a while until Betty asked what Goulding wanted and he turned his attention to her.

'Pint please love.'

He turned and surveyed the rest of the room. Walt and Jack had left as soon as they saw him enter leaving two unfinished drinks on the table. He took in the domino players nodded to them then picked up his pint and sat at the table by the wall where Wath and Coleen had chatted. It gave him a full view of the room and meant that if Wath continued talking to Betty he would be in Wath's eyeline constantly.

Trying to ignore Goulding who was deliberately staring at him Wath turned his attention to Betty. 'I'm going to Aldwick Steel Foundry in Parkgate tomorrow. There's a chance of some work. Fancy coming with me and we can go into Rotherham after?'

Betty's smiled broadened. 'Aye. What time?'

'Well, I've got an appointment at one thirty so if we leave here just before one that should be fine. But you might have to sit in the lorry for a while as I talk to them.'

'Okay. Can we go round the market? It's been ages since I've done that.'

'Sure, look Goulding is trying to wind me up and succeeding. I'm going home, I'll pick you up at the bridge at five to one tomorrow.'

Betty beamed as Wath drained his pint. Goulding was only half way down his and neither man acknowledged the other as Wath left. Betty however glared at Goulding - he had almost cleared her bar without saying a word.

Returning to Treacle Town it was too early to go to bed and Wath was feeling nervy, unsettled. Goulding had rattled him. He needed activity. He went upstairs and looked in his mother's bedroom. It was pretty much as he had found it. A mess.

143

He gathered all her clothes, stripped the bed and stuffed everything into a sack. He stood for a while looking at the empty room then decided. Taking the sack downstairs, he pulled the spare sheet and blanket from the sideboard and fitted them on the bed. He fluffed up the pillows and found a spare pillowcase in his mother's wardrobe. Once again, he stood for a long time looking at the bed.

He sat on the edge, the mattress surprising him by bouncing slightly.

It had been a long time.

He took his shoes off and sat again. He puffed up the pillow realising he was deliberately delaying. Gingerly he lay down. A train went past on the GCR line its noise echoing around the empty room, the house rocking slightly as it rolled by with its rhythmic ker clunk, ker clunk. A coke oven flare cast its light into the night and the room brightened. His heart was thudding against his chest, he felt nauseous, he was sweating. Wath stood and closed the curtains. Looking down at the bed one last time he picked up his shoes and walked downstairs, wrapped himself in his blankets in his chair and fell fast asleep.

Chapter Twenty Four

Wednesday 13/4/1920

Henry sat watching the men opposite him. Smedley and Goulding had questioned him and his men mercilessly since the robbery and here they were again. Items from the compound had been used in the pit wages heist and every member of staff had been interrogated over and over again with their stories cross checked repeatedly and those who had no alibi for the morning of the ninth of April had their homes raided and their families questioned. As yet no one had been charged but Henry was now angry.

This was the last straw.

Smedley was sat in his office accusing him of conniving with or at the very least covering up for Wath Dyson. He took his time answering.

'I have no time or respect for that man, but the haulier with the contract, Joe Whiteley, wanted to quit and he wanted to hand the contract to Dyson. I could have refused but it would have meant seeking a new haulier at a very difficult time with all the planned strikes and uncertainties regarding the pits. So, despite my dislike of the man, I made a commercial decision and yes I gave him a contract to enable him to buy a lorry.'

Smedley watched him keenly. 'Before the robbery.'

'You've seen the contract. Yes, before the robbery.'

'Thank you, Mr Mallinder. We may be back with more questions. Oh, by the way – you do know that your new haulier is a convict don't you.'

'What!'

'Didn't he tell you. Oh dear, well perhaps you should ask him.'

'Wait. You tell me. He wouldn't tell me if I begged him.'

Smedley looked across the huge table a cunning gleam in his eye.

'He served twelve months of an eighteen-month sentence in the Army Prison for starting a riot. He only got out the month before last.'

Henry sat immersed in his own thoughts. Oblivious to the men opposite.

'Anyway, Good day Mr Mallinder. Thank you for your assistance.'

Henry watched the two men leave. Dyson had been in jail. Had he known that earlier he would have refused Lucy's request to let him see Alice and there was no way he would have transferred the contract. He thought about Coleen. Would she have known. Would she still ask him to pass on the contract; probably. She was cunning that one and evil. He couldn't risk upsetting her. He would carry on with the agreement – for now.

Smedley grinned conspiratorially at Goulding. 'You're right. Dyson is involved in this somehow. Let's keep the pressure on. You keep in his face, keep letting him see you but don't provoke him.'

'My pleasure.'

'I'm going to Doncaster to speak with the Lorry Salesman and the Pawnbroker. We'll meet up tomorrow.'

Smedley walked into Mexborough and caught the train to Doncaster. The Salesman showed him all the correct paperwork and gave a statement that Dyson had acted correctly at all times. Next Smedley sought out the pawnbroker. As he entered a young woman was stood behind the counter and she brought out the owner Winfield.

'Good afternoon how can I help?'

'I would like to ask a few questions. My name is Smedley, Detective Smedley and I am investigating a robbery.' The man behind the counter nodded, pawnbrokers were used to questions from the police.

'Do you know a man called Wath Dyson?'

'Yes. I gave him a loan to buy an automobile, a lorry.'

'Can I see the paperwork?'

'Yes. Just one moment.'

Winfield disappeared back through the door and returned a minute later with a sheaf of papers. Standing in front of the counter he placed the papers on top, passing them one by one to Smedley.

'Is there a problem Detective?'

'It's just such a large amount to borrow so close to a robbery.'

'And if there was no robbery, would you still be asking questions?'

Smedley hesitated looking up from the agreement. He didn't answer which he realised was answer enough.

'So how is Dyson linked to the robbery?'

'There is no physical link it's just his past.'

'You looked into his past?'

Smedley was uncomfortable. Somehow this interview was out of control. Winfield was asking the questions and he was the one being interviewed 'Some, he was in jail.'

'Ahh his jail sentence. Wait there please detective.'

Winfield went behind the counter and opened a large safe. From inside he took a box which he opened, placing a row of medals and newspaper cuttings on the counter.

'These are Mr Dysons medals. He sold them to me on his return. I have investigated how he won the medals and, I can assure you detective, that man has done more for this country then the rest of this city put together. Were you in the war?'

'Yes.'

'On the front line?'

'Staff Headquarters.'

'Well look at these medals detective. You will know how hard it is to earn these and the prison sentence… he stopped an officer assaulting one of his men. It caused a riot. The officer got off scot free but Dyson was charged and spent twelve months in jail. In my

147

opinion that was wrong. So, when the young man came to me looking for a loan I said yes. He wants to turn his life around detective and I hope he takes his chance. If my loan helps him then I will be satisfied but as a business man I am also making profit in the form of interest. You detective are hounding him because of his past and a dubious prison sentence. Find your villains detective but do not come back here.

'Good bye detective.'

Winfield wrapped the medals and cuttings back in the box and returned them to the safe. He did not look up as the Detective left the shop.

Smedley walked to the corner and sat on a bench in the park opposite. He pulled out his pipe and for the first time in several weeks lit it. He had never experienced anything like that. He was glad Goulding wasn't there to see it. There was something telling him that Dyson was involved but that wasn't a brick wall he had just run into; it was a train hurtling down the track and he had been dragged under the wheels.

And there was more, his neighbour had seen him just half an hour after the robbery. It was a full two miles by road from where the attack happened to where he lived – through a colliery. It was impossible for him to get home unseen in that time and the signal man had witnessed him in the yard.

Then the man who hated him the most, who had sent men to beat him up, the man who stole his girlfriend while he was at war confirmed the issue of a haulage contract nearly three weeks before the robbery and the salesman backed him and now the pawnbroker. Then according to Goulding every single person in the local pub confirmed he had bragged about the purchase and the loan well before the robbery.

Every one - everything - told him the man was innocent.

But Smedley scented blood.

Lucy cleared the plates in no time, there was only her and Alice having an early dinner. It was the second Wednesday in April, time for Henry's monthly Masonic meeting and he was due to leave any minute. Lucy washed the pots listening to Henry who was on a rant. They were quite frequent at the moment but this one was enlightening. Two policemen had been to the factory and questioned Henry – again. Henry was furious but he let slip that they had accused Wath of being in prison. According to what she could divine from Henry's rant Wath had started a riot and been incarcerated on his return to England.

Why hadn't he told her?

What had happened?

She couldn't ask Henry as he would blow and he was already bristling with anger but Wath and prisons were like two sides of the same coin. Close to one another yet never likely to meet.

Lucy walked down the hill with Henry and Alice and, leaving him at the bottom of the road to go to his meeting, she and her daughter turned off to visit her parents. As quickly as she could she dropped Alice with her mother promising to be back in a couple of hours at the most and marched along the canal to Common Lane.

At the top she strode down into Treacle Town and knocked on Wath's door. There was no answer. She stood uncertain, listening to the rumbles in the pit yard as wagons were shunted. It was all very familiar, even the smell. Turning she saw Frank in the signal box waving to her, she waved back and went up to see him.

At least the smell would be reduced up there.

'You look well,' he said, 'after Wath?'

'Yeah,' she took her coat off and hung it over one of the levers, 'just wanted to clear something up.'

Frank watched the face, the way the end of her pert nose moved as she talked. Every time he saw her, he was reminded of how pretty she was.

'For God's sake don't accuse him of robbery, he's had enough of that.'

'No. Not that, besides I heard it was an armed gang. Wath is a lone wolf, never been in a gang. Did you know he was sent to jail when he came back to England?'

Frank held his breath, stunned into silence. He stared at Lucy for a long few seconds not knowing what to say. If Wath wanted people to know he would tell them. It wasn't Frank's place to interfere.

'It's ok you've just confirmed it. Two policemen went to see Henry today and told him Wath'd been jailed for starting a riot.'

'Lucy, you know what Wath's like, he don't want to talk about the war. He burned his uniform and sold his medals the first day he got back. Said he would never talk about it again.'

'Medals?'

'Oh shit. Yeah medals. He won several and was promoted. But he won't tell anyone. Won't talk about it. A part of his life he wants to forget.'

'Christ the mans a bloody enigma. Why can't he just be like normal people, why did I have to fall in love with him of all people' she stared at Frank. He'd seen her life during the war years. Knew what she had gone through. Tears started to well in her eyes. 'Why did I have to live in silence for nearly four years?'

Frustration oozed and Frank stayed silent but at that moment a lorry pulled around the corner and Wath stepped out moving towards the house. Lucy grabbed her coat, shouted 'Thanks Frank.' and raced through the door. Frank sighed, he hoped she wouldn't tear into him and he hoped Wath would talk to her.

Wath was just closing the door when Lucy shouted. He stopped, paralysed, as she walked up without saying anything else then stepped past him into the kitchen. She scrutinised the room. 'Well, you've certainly improved the old place.' She said as sarcastically as she could. The walls were still the same old shades of brown and cream, a dado and picture rail both empty, nothing on the floor. Two chairs at the table, an armchair with blankets on it, a sideboard at the back of the room and everything else functional.

Wath shrugged. 'Other than police or debt collectors you're the first person inside since I got back.'

She threw her coat over the back of a chair, sat on it and pushed back looking at him.

'You seem to be making a start with the lorry.'

'Aye.'

'What's going off Wath? Goulding and another policeman have told Henry you were in jail. Is it true?'

Wath moved over to the stove and grabbed the kettle. 'Brew?'

'Answer?'

He smiled she had always been direct. He put the kettle on and leant back against the sink. The enamel at his back vibrated as a train passed on the GCR line.

'Aye. I was in jail.'

'Why?'

He sighed, reluctant to speak but realised she would press until she found out. Best get it over with. 'Officer hit one of my men. I hit the officer. It started a fight and I was blamed.'

'That's it?'

'Well, a couple of buildings got burnt down and a couple of officers hospitalised.' As if by command a flare rose from the coke ovens lighting the back drop behind him giving his outline a sinister hue.

'Why was he hitting your man?'

'Cos, he wanted to go home.'

'Why didn't you tell me?'

'I wasn't allowed to write and when I got back, I could hardly say I'm late because I've been in jail could I. Henry would've been in his eye holes.'

'They wouldn't let you write?' he nodded in reply, 'What about before then?'

What could he say? There was no real explanation, other men managed it. But killing, surviving, obeying, winning, they became all consuming. Everything else forgotten, deliberately locked away.

'Remember when I came back off leave for training. When I went back late. Well, they gave me field punishment number two. Put me in chains for twenty-one days. They shipped me across to France in chains. When I got sent up to the trenches there was a soldier chained to a post. In the trenches. That was field punishment number one. He'd written home and told his Missus where he was stationed - that's a criminal offence in the Army. I'd already done number two so was certain of number one if I did anything wrong and you know how bad my writing used to be.'

He could see she found his excuse limp. To be fair so did he.

'You got promoted.'

'Lucy, I don't want to talk about the war. I've done with it. It's behind me.'

She completely ignored him. The only sign she had heard him was an increase in the gruffness of her voice. 'Why didn't we know you'd been promoted?'

'You did. My wages went up.'

'Your mothers drinking went up. She collected the money from the post office, gave me five shillings a week. Never changed the whole time.'

He was shocked. He should have never put his mother on his form. The money should have gone to Lucy. She would have known of his promotions, used the money wisely, who knows she might even still be waiting for him.

'Sorry.'

'You're at it again. Apologising.'

'Sorry.' It came out instinctively. They both laughed.

'You'll be seeing me and Alice soon.'

'Aye. Looking forward to it.'

'So am I... Wath you know I can't leave Henry. Don't you?'

He sat silent.

'You know I can't bring Alice back to this.' She waved her arm around the room. He knew but hearing it was hard. She looked at him questioningly.

152

He nodded.

He knew.

Lucy watched him silently, contemplating her next words. Her decision made she stood up and turned, lifting her hair from her neck with both hands. 'Would you mind undoing my buttons.' Wath trembled as he fumbled the back of her dress open. She allowed it to fall to the floor then bent down and picked it up. Holding it in front of her she moved to the bottom of the stairs. 'I've only got an hour.' He followed behind.

Watching Lucy walk up Common Lane Wath realised he was going to be late. When he dropped her off, he had arranged to meet Betty in the Nelson after she had made her dad dinner. He jogged back into the yard and opened the oil can he used to top up the lorry. Wiping some oil into his hands he set off to the pub. Pushing his way inside, Betty was already sat at his table talking with Walt and Jack.

'Where've you been?'

'I thought the lorry had an oil leak, had to check. Sorry. Got here as quick as I could' he turned to the bar and ordered a pint from the landlord who only served when Betty was off duty 'got an old rag or something Doug. Something I can wipe my hands on. Didn't have time back there.'

Doug pulled out an old beer towel which Wath took to the table along with another Mackeson for Betty. Wiping his hands fastidiously he sat down. Betty pulled a face 'You think more of that lorry than you do of me.'

'Might do if it pulled pints as well as you do.'

Bill overheard and joined in 'He's got a point Betty love. Bet Doug's takings are down by half when you're not behind the bar.

Betty smiled and picked up her drink, Wath's lateness forgotten. Wath breathed a sigh of relief and mentally thanked Bill for his comment as he took a long swallow of desperately needed beer.

The conversation drifted around him as he reviewed the past hour. Lucy had said that she could not bring Alice back to Treacle Town and he understood. But then she went upstairs. Was that for old times sake? A goodbye? He was confused but there was one certainty inside all the mist; he needed Lucy more than ever. He must make his haulage business work. He had to create the environment she craved but would that be enough? What would she come back to?

She said she could not leave Henry. A feeling of depression sank over him. He was dreaming, Lucy was never coming back her life was too comfortable with Henry. He sighed, ordered more beers and re-joined the conversation.

A couple of hours later they left the pub and Wath walked Betty home. Outside the door of the terrace she shared with her father she stopped 'Want to come in for a cup of tea?'

'What about your dad?'

'He's on nights. Come on I'll not eat yer alive.'

She opened the door and Wath followed her through. Waiting until he had passed, she closed the door behind him. Catching him completely by surprise she grabbed hold of him and pushed him back against the door. Pinning him there with her body she put both her hands around his neck pulling his face onto hers 'But then again I might.' She said, crushing his lips with hers.

Chapter Twenty Five

Saturday 17/4/1920

Smalley kept glancing over but Wath ignored him. He leant back against the station wall and watched the cloud of smoke and steam making its way up the track. Smalley did his flag waving theatrics and the train glided to a halt at its precise arrival time of twenty past three. Patrick was the first out and he turned to help Coleen from the carriage. She smiled as she saw Wath and walked across. Patrick moved towards the baggage carriage where a group of men were gathered pulling cases off the train.

Pushing her arm through Wath's Coleen said, 'Come on then boy. I'm looking forward to this.' They left Patrick behind and walked at a comfortable pace through Wath upon Dearne. Approaching the pheasantry up Fitzwilliam Street they could see Lucy and Alice outside waiting for them. Stopping in front of the house the two women looked at each other, both making their own private assessment. Alice looked at Wath.

'What are we going to do today?'

'I want you to meet a friend of mine.'

'Who?'

'Jewel.'

'Jewel? That's a funny name.'

'Jewel is a horse and me and her are the best of friends but I haven't given her apples yet this week and I thought you might like to do it for me.'

'Yes please. Get in. Mam we're going to feed Jewel, come on let's go.'

Alice grabbed Wath's hand and started to march away. Lucy and Coleen shrugged and fell in behind chatting as they walked.

When they got to Orchard Place, Jewel was out in the field and Wath called her over. Tentatively at first Alice fed the horse the apples and the horse nuzzled her affectionately. Coleen leant across and scratched the horse behind the ear. Jewel responded immediately seeking more from Coleen but when Lucy approached the horse backed off.

Coleen laughed 'You should spend some time on a farm, you two wait there. Come on Alice let's see if Jewel will give you a ride.'

Wath and Lucy stood by the fence while Coleen led the horse around for a while getting her comfortable, then with surprisingly little effort Coleen persuaded Jewel to allow Alice to sit on her back. The girl was delighted. After a while they left Jewel and walked through the Grange around Abdy and back to Fitzwilliam Street via Newhill. It had only been two hours but Lucy wanted the sessions to start slowly and build up comfortably. Wath would have agreed to anything and he knew she was right as he walked away with the young girl's words 'Can we do that again?' ringing in his ears.

His cheeks were aching with smiling as he and Coleen reached the High Street and turned towards Manvers and Treacle Town.

'So, what is it with you and the girl's mother?'

'She left me while I was at war.'

'Are you sure?'

'What's that mean?'

'There were sparks flying between you two. Every time I came between you the static made my hair stand on end.'

Coleen waited but Wath remained silent.

'I can understand why Henry doesn't like you. He must be jealous stiff. That woman can't take her eyes off you.'

Again, Wath answered with silence.

At the top of Common Lane Coleen said 'I fancy a drink – are you having one?'

'Aye.'

156

They entered the Nelson and sat at the side of the domino table. Coleen with her usual whiskey and Wath with his pint. Bill and Syd could hardly take their eyes off Coleen while Betty kept watch from the bar. Coleen studied the dominoes then turned to Wath.

'What do you reckon boy, do you think we could beat these at their own game?'

'No chance. I'm sure them dominoes are marked.'

'Come on let's give them a game.'

'Coleen I've had the best day of my life, let's not spoil it by losing to them.'

'Come on. Where's your spirit, you're on a roll. Let's batter them.'

Bill and Syd overheard the conversation and after a few minutes of light hearted banter Coleen and Wath swopped places with Tom and Ted and shuffled the dominoes.

'Now then,' she said 'straight dominoes none o that fives and threes rubbish.'

'What are we playing for?' barked Syd.

'Losers buy the next round.' Coleen replied as Wath groaned, he'd lost enough money at dominoes.

Bill could not keep the smile from his face 'You're on.'

They shuffled the dominoes and after one quick look at each domino Coleen placed hers face down, not touching them or turning them over until she played them into the table. Inside five minutes Coleen had both Bill and Syd knocking as she seemed able to predict every domino they had. Wath thought he coped but withering looks or crushing smiles told him if he was playing the right domino or not.

As they played Betty came from behind the bar and stood behind Wath watching the game with an arm draped possessively across his shoulder. There was a resigned silence and black mood from Bill and Syd as Coleen played her last domino. They knew what was happening. This tied up both ends and a count back revealed Bill and Syd lost by two points.

157

They were crestfallen. Coleen howled, slapping her knee in delight.

'Betty get back behind that bar and start pouring our drinks. These are going to be the sweetest tasting drinks we'll ever drink.'

'It's normally the best of three games.' pouted Syd.

'Not today my lovely. I hereby retire from dominoes the undefeated champion. Come on Wath let's celebrate.'

Laughing at Bill and Syd, Coleen moved across to the far table where, after collecting their drinks, Wath joined her. As they sat down without any preamble she asked 'What's with Betty then?'

'What do you mean?'

'Arm across the shoulder.'

'She's a close friend.'

'Careful boy, women can be awfully vengeful and three into two definitely doesn't go.'

Wath broke into a grin 'Want to tell you to shut up, but got to say I'm enjoying your concern. Never had anybody but Frank worry about me before.'

'Frank?'

'The man in the signal box.'

'Do you go in there often?'

'Almost lived up there when I was younger. Used to operate it for them.'

'So, you know how it all works.'

'Aye. Can tell the time of day by the service coming past. Can tell you where the train is going by which signal changes at which time. Living in Treacle Town you're surrounded by it, you just know what's going on, becomes second nature.'

'We might need a serious talk. I might need a favour from you.'

'Anytime. Today was brilliant and I've got a lorry, so I owe you.'

At that point Patrick walked in. 'Ready Coleen?'

'To be sure.' She finished her drink.

'Is that it, are you leaving, going back to Dublin?'

158

'No, we're going to stay for a couple o days.'

'Where are you staying?'

'Not sure, Patricks been making the arrangements, but I'll see you before I go. Promise.' She stood up as Patrick left the pub, kissed the inside of her fingers on her right hand and placed the kiss on Wath's cheek. 'It was a good day for me too.'

Chapter Twenty Six

After they left Wath moved across the pub and joined Jimmy at his usual table. Jimmy had been to a union conference that afternoon and was on his soap box yet again. Once he had finished explaining the intricacies of mining unions to young Jack, they called it a day and headed home. Walking down Common Lane at a pace controlled by Jimmy's limp they became aware that something was wrong, there was the sound of an argument inside Treacle Town. They looked at each other, they were the only residents and they were outside.

Approaching the Signal Box Wath stopped when he thought he saw smoke coming from the Jenkinson's chimney. Frank saw them approaching and waved at them from inside the box, urging them to hurry.

Turning the corner, there was a line of men strung across the yard with Patrick stood out in front. Facing them was Goulding in off duty clothes. An argument was raging and both men were squaring up to each other.

'What is he up to now and what are they doing here?' demanded Jimmy.

Wath didn't answer instead he ran into the yard and jumped in between the two men just as Patrick was throwing his first punch. Catching them by surprise he shouldered Goulding out of the way, took Patrick's punch across his shoulders then pushed him hard in the chest. Patrick staggered while Goulding stumbled back to his feet. Wath stood between the two of them his arms out wide holding them at bay.

'Stop! What's going off.'

'I'm gunna whip his arse.' yelled Goulding.

'Don't be stupid Goulding. What's going off Patrick?'

'We caught him snooping, trying to look in your window.'

'Goulding?'

'I was looking for you.'

'You knew where I was.'

'And he was crawling all over your lorry. Reckon he was trying to nick it when he knew you weren't in.'

Wath shook his head. 'He's a policeman Patrick, he wasn't trying to steal.'

'Yeah, well he's still going to get a beating. He called me a thick Irish pansy.'

'Yer nothing but bog dwelling slime.' spat Goulding.

Wath pushed him back, waving his arms. 'Shut the fuck up Goulding, can't you see there's an army of them.'

'I only want him.'

'For Christs sake man, leave it.' Wath turned back to Patrick who was advancing again. 'Get back Patrick.'

'I'm for smashing him.'

'He's a copper!'

'So fecking what.'

'Hit him and they'll flood the place.'

'Get out o the way.'

'Ok, if that's the way you want it but to get to him, you're gunna have to go through me.'

'What?'

'That's just the way it is. He's a copper. You're not beating up a copper on my doorstep.'

'Don't make me hit you boy.'

'Then back off.'

Jimmy came up and stood at the other side of Goulding.

Patrick burst out laughing. 'Look at this, a one-armed cripple, a thieving copper and a pick pocketing coward. The very best of England are lined up against us boys.' The men behind him laughed as they started to move forward.

'Stop!'

161

Coleen moved off the step from where she had been watching the scene develop. 'Patrick stop. You' she faced Goulding 'get out o here now. There'll be no fight. Back inside lads. We're not to attack policemen. Not today. Come on now. As I say.'

The men slowly backed off. Patrick and Goulding stood glaring at each other before Coleen walked in between them and pushed Patrick back. 'Go on Patrick there'll be other times.'

'I'll get you.' He spat at Golding.

'Next time your arse is mine sunshine.'

'Leave it Goulding. Let's call this over.' Said Wath pushing him gently back towards the signal box. Frank joined the three of them as they regrouped at the bottom of the signal box steps.

'You alright?' Frank asked Wath.

'Aye. What's been going off Frank?'

'Don't know. About six or seven men came this afternoon and started to break into the end two terraces. Like they were going to live there. The big one left and came back with a woman. Is that Coleen? Then they all went inside and Goulding appears. He looks in through your window, then starts to inspect your lorry and they all tumble out of the house and start to argue. That's when you turned up.'

'Goulding?'

'Sounds about right.'

'What were you after?'

'You. You robbed them wages and I'm going to prove it.'

'Jesus you just don't know when to give up.'

'And I'll not. Not til I've got you lad.' Goulding turned and marched away.

'Well, there's a grateful bugger.' muttered Jimmy.

They all watched as Goulding turned the corner and started up the Lane. His thick legs pumping in time while his arms swung as if on parade.

'Would you really have fought for him?' Frank asked.

Wath sighed 'Aye. If he'd been beaten up, there would have been coppers all over here for the next week and do you know what... somehow, I would have been blamed' he looked back into the now silent yard 'but truthfully, I was relying on Coleen stopping it before it went too far. Anyway, that's enough entertainment for one night. I'm going to bed. See you two tomorrow.'

Walking though the yard he took in the scene. The boarding to the Jenkinson's and the terrace next to it had been pulled off and both doors were open. A man was sat on the step of each house as if on guard and he could hear the muffled talk of others inside. He tried to act nonchalant but knew he was failing. He said good night and walked on.

Closing the kitchen door behind him, he leant back against it.

What was happening?

He had been certain that no one would go inside the Jenkinson's but Coleen! He opened his tool bag and pulled out a screwdriver and two screws. Within five minutes he had the loft hatch screwed shut.

He stoked the fire and sat looking into the flames. He did a mental count of how much money was left in the Jenkinson's coal cellar. He had managed to deposit five hundred pounds into the various bank accounts in total. There was a further one hundred pounds ready to be deposited, hidden under the fire grate in the front room. Ignoring the two hundred pounds in five-pound notes he thought there was still over nine hundred pounds left.

Left?

It was gone.

The smoke coming from the Jenkinson's chimney as they entered the yard was real. That could only mean someone had been down the cellar to get coal and he had made no effort to hide the bags.

He put the kettle on and made himself tea. He tried to calm down. Panic would not help but he felt it closing in. A crash from the coke oven retort echoed and the house vibrated gently as a train passed. The comfort blanket of Treacle Town wrapped itself around him. He would just have to forget the rest of the money. He had what he wanted. That was enough. Move on.

Decision made and resolve hardened he poured himself a mug of tea.

A feminine knock sounded on the door and Coleen walked in. She didn't say a word, just sat at the table, placed a pair of goggles in front of her then reached across and took the mug he had poured for himself and drank from it. Wath felt a chill move up his back.

Her face was different, a new expression firming the lips, an aurora of control seemed to make her glow. It was his mind playing tricks, his mood painting pictures for his imagination, he knew it was the reflection from the coke oven flares framing her outline. But still his unease grew.

They sat in silence until eventually Coleen said 'Want to tell me about it?'

'No.'

'You don't deny it?'

'Deny what?'

She smiled. 'How much was the lorry?'

'Eight hundred pounds.'

'The receipts say two thousand six hundred so I reckon you spent well over half. Here's what we're going to do. If you help me, I'll keep my mouth shut. If you don't, I'm going to go tell that copper what we've found.'

'You wouldn't.'

'I would... but you won't risk that. You'll help me.'

'What do you want?'

'I want to derail a train.'

'Now I could go to Goulding.'

'But you won't.'

164

Chapter Twenty Seven

Monday 19/4/1920

His first pickup was at eight o clock so Wath had a gentle start to the morning. Whenever he ventured outside there was an Irishman sat on the step of one of the two end houses. They were definitely on guard and it felt unsettling. Eventually he took the money from the front room and the paperwork for the lorry putting them in the inside pocket of his jacket then left the house. Once outside, for the first time he could remember, he locked the door behind him. As he turned, he was greeted by a leering Patrick. 'That'll not stop us if we want to get in.'

He ignored him and walked to the lorry.

'Coleen wants a meeting, what time will you be back.'

'When I've finished.'

'Don't get cocky boy. She doesn't like cocky.'

Once again Wath ignored him, started the lorry and pulled out of the yard. As he got to the signal box Smedley was running down the steps, waving. He stopped and waited.

'Need a chat.'

'Busy, got a collection at eight.'

'Can you talk while you drive?' Wath shrugged. 'Then let me ride with you. We'll chat on the way.' Smedley jumped up into the cab on the passenger side and sat with a smile on his face. 'Let's see what eight hundred pounds buys.'

Wath drove up Common Lane and turned towards Wath upon Dearne and West Melton. He was due to collect sand from West Field Farm and deliver it to Twentieth Century Concrete. For a while Smedley kept quiet, watching Wath drive and the scenery move past. But his silence didn't last long.

'What happened Saturday night?'

'Goulding picked a fight.'

'You intervened.' When there was no answer, he continued. 'On Goulding's side.'

'He would've been battered, then you lot would've been all over Treacle Town.'

'Ah, now I understand. Self-preservation. What're the Irish doing?'

'Honestly no idea. But once Suggett hears he'll be on their case.'

'Suggett?'

'The Landlords rent collector.'

'Your story checked out.'

Again, there was a long silence. 'The Pawnbroker seems to have taken a liking to you.'

Wath shrugged.

'Why him not the Banks?'

'The Banks don't like Treacle Town.'

'Add me to that list.'

Another long silence ensued as Wath navigated the lorry through Townend and into West Melton.

'The Banks tell me you don't pay rent.'

'That's right.'

'How do you get away with that?'

Wath considered ignoring the question but decided telling the detective would do no harm.

'When me Mam died Suggett went through the house, took everything of value. I got back before he boarded up. Told him he'd had enough from us and I wouldn't be paying a penny. Told him any argument bring his bosses to see me. Not paid a penny since.'

'You could report him for theft.'

'Aye and watch Goulding mess it up and then end up paying rent. Thanks, but no thanks.'

It was Smedley's turn for silence as they arrived at West Field Farm. Wath supervised and helped with the loading of the sand before they started back at a much-reduced pace.

166

'Does it bother you?'

'What?'

'The farm. If not for the murders that would be yours eventually.'

'No Smedley, it does not bother me. I learnt long ago never look back and never dream about what could have been. For years my only concern was survival.'

'The War?'

'No. Life.'

'What was prison like?'

Wath slammed the brakes on and pulled in to the side of the road.

'Think you ought to get out now.'

'Only trying to get to know you.'

'Don't bother. Smedley… I've known lots of police in my time and none of them have ever done me any favours. All of them wanted me lashed or behind bars. You're no different. At least Goulding is up front about it. I'd like you to get out now please. I've had enough.'

Smedley climbed out of the cab and stood at the curb side. Wath engaged the gears and moved smoothly away. Smedley watched the lorry disappear into the distance.

A little after six Wath pulled back into the yard and climbed out of the lorry. Before he had walked three paces Patrick was on him.

'Coleen wants that meeting. Now.'

Wath held up a package wrapped in newspaper. 'Got my dinner. Fish and chips, I'll be having that first.'

Patrick glared at him. 'She'll be around in fifteen minutes.'

Making a pot of tea Wath ate his meal and threw the paper onto the fire where the fat on it burned with a satisfying flare. Watching it burn he wondered what he was heading into. He had accepted the loss of the money but what would Coleen demand for her silence.

167

Derailing a train was easy it was just which train. Most of the services locally were goods trains, most carrying over five hundred tons of cargo and the damage they caused when they left the track was frightening. But he felt trapped.

The flames from the fat ripped up the chimney burning the soot at the back of the fireplace. A red glow settled there when the flames died down and Wath watched, subconsciously trying to find a pattern, trying to make sense of the chaos in the flames and embers. There was none but he was lost to the world as the door opened and Coleen walked in.

'Is there a spare cup o tea available?'

Pouring her one he sat opposite her at the table, cradling his mug in his hands, waiting. She was in control and they both knew it.

'Okay, I think we've established a measure o trust. You didn't tell the detective about our plans and we didn't tell Goulding about your little escapade. But I need to know that you're fully in. The men don't like it, me trusting you.'

'I'm in, but I only help with the planning. I do not do any of the spade work. I want to be miles away when this happens.'

'You'll only be involved in the planning. Are we agreed?'

Reluctantly Wath nodded his head 'Aye.'

'There is one further thing. This train we want derailing. If you don't play your part in planning or you breathe one word to anybody there will be consequences and it won't be just you.'

'Don't threaten me Coleen, I don't respond well to threats.'

'Yer must know that we'll take revenge if you talk?'

'Aye.'

'So, I'm just making sure you understand.'

They stared at each other, a hardness glazing Coleen's eyes the like of which Wath had never seen on a woman. The only time he had seen the stare before was on men about to go over the top. It was the glare of a zealot, someone who had convinced themselves that what they were doing was right. Even though they knew the cost. Even when the cost was everything. She held his stare and raised a finger, pointing at him.

'If you break your word it won't be you I'll be leaving on the gravestone next time but one o your females.'

She meant it. There was no doubt in her voice, no flicker in her expression. Every single fibre of her body was behind the statement. He felt a shiver but held the stare.

'That's not the way to get my co-operation.'

'Oh, I believe it is. Think about it. I'll be back in an hour.'

Chapter Twenty Eight

Monday 19/4/1920

She sat at the table with another man. Much younger with wild curly black hair. He was thin almost anaemic and wore spectacles which gave him a studious air. Patrick and two other large men stood up, leaning on the sideboard at the back of the room. The room shrank as Wath realised this was probably the largest gathering it had ever seen.

As usual Coleen took charge. 'Before I start, I want everyone in the room to know what we've agreed' she pointed at Wath 'you will help us, give us advice on the movement o trains and help with the planning. You will not be involved in the execution o our plans. In return we will not reveal your little escapade to the police. You will not speak one word o our plans to anyone outside this room.'

'Coleen, I want everyone to know, including him,' said Patrick pointing at Wath 'that I'm not happy with him being involved.'

'We've been through this Patrick and it is my decision.'

Patrick nodded. 'He needs to know and he needs to know what will happen if he talks.'

'I think he's already worked that bit out.'

Wath watched the exchange knowing it was an act for his benefit. Even the performance earlier by Coleen was staged. It didn't take a genius to work out the consequences of him reneging on their agreement. Derailing a train was an act of terrorism. They would do anything to hide their tracks.

He wasn't bothered about himself, he could handle Patrick, but the threat to Lucy and Betty had ramped the pressure up. He could not protect them both, not at the same time.

'Right. Liam get the maps out, let's start.'

The young academic unrolled a map. It was a standard government issue map of Wath upon Dearne and the surrounding area. There were long black scars on it showing all the railway lines linking buildings, factories and mines and in the middle a small block of housing indicating Treacle Town. Liam leant forward pointing at the map but looking at and talking to Wath.

'This is the MNER line, it runs all the way from London up to York. We want to derail a train on this track. We want to derail it as it crosses this ground here,' he pointed at an area on the map described as marsh land and designated as Low Common 'at this point the tracks are raised on an embankment and a derailment here will cause the carriages to fall down the embankment causing the most damage to the train but they will land in fields so minimum damage to locals.'

Liam looked at Wath for confirmation. 'Go on.' he said.

'We want your opinion on how to do it. The train passes through on Friday and we can't get any explosives here in time so it must be done by other means. I thought we could loosen a rail or interfere with a signal point but it's where and when.'

'Which train are you targeting. If it's a goods train it'll be a lot heavier and moving slower than a passenger service.'

'It's a passenger service.'

Wath drew his breath in. Sensing his mood Coleen interrupted 'It's a special service, it's not a schedule service.'

He waited, staring at her.

'It's the Royal train.'

'What! Are you crazy? You want to derail the Royal train! Bugger me…' he threw his hands into the air '…. even if no one is killed the police, the army, they'll swamp this place for weeks.'

'So fecking what. Catholics are being attacked in Ulster. The British are burning our towns—'

'— you ambush soldiers.'

'Who kill our young men—'

'— and you lot are innocent victims'

'Innocent victims: you want innocent victims, seven thousand Catholics thrown out o their jobs in Belfast, just last week.'

171

'My heart bleeds for yer.'

'It should, the British swamp us. Spies everywhere. It's hard to move in Ireland. This is a chance to hit back… on English soil.'

'It's an act of terror is what it is.'

'It's an act o war. Ireland is at war.'

'I'm not Irish.'

'I warned you Coleen.'

'Shut up Patrick. You've got my blood in you. Look my husband was murdered, my son is in jail—'

'— your husband was executed.'

'Yes, for his beliefs.'

'For murder.'

'For wanting a free Ireland' Coleen was now red in the face, sweating, her passion, her beliefs on the line 'the British done you no favours. You've been lashed, locked up and sent to war what do you owe them?'

Wath stayed silent. He could not argue that point. His life had been one long struggle against authority. A fight with the system. Coleen pushed back from the table and scowled at him.

'I told you earlier what the consequences are. They apply as o now. All of the consequences. What do you want to do pretty boy?'

She had made her stance.

It was now his decision.

Wath stared. She was in front of him but he didn't see her. His eyes were focused internally – on consequences. His temples throbbed. He was angry, frustrated. But trapped. He had never felt like this before. Responsible for innocents, for Lucy and Betty, who had no idea what was happening but would suffer the fallout of his failure. He decided to bargain, it was all he had left.

'I want your word that neither Lucy or Betty will be harmed if I agree to go through with this.'

'They will not, you have my word.'

He nodded 'Then I'll do it.'

'But if you break yours the boys will take their time with you.'

'You can have my word on that.' interrupted Patrick from the back of the room.

Wath ripped his eyes from Coleen and turned to look at Patrick. The two men alongside were smiling triumphantly with him. Frustration roared to the front of his head. He could not hold himself back.

'Goulding was right, you're one fuck of a gobshite. At least Ulstermen know how to fight. I saw that at the Somme. You lot are only good for murdering men in their beds, shaving women's heads and throwing petrol bombs from behind walls. You'll never get independence.'

All the smiles disappeared. Patrick pushed himself from the wall. Coleen held her hand up to stop him and leant into the table glaring at Wath.

'But we might pretty boy, we just might… if we attack the Royal train in the middle o England. So… tell us how we do it.'

Wath stared at the map on the table. He ignored Patrick taking deep breaths behind him. He turned to the young man, Liam, who had watched the drama unfold around him without a flicker of emotion.

'Tell me everything you know.'

The spectacles reflected the last rays of light from outside, stopping Wath seeing the eyes but a long lock of hair swung in front of them as the young man bobbed his head. Happy to be moving on.

'Prince Albert has been made the Duke o York. On Friday he goes up to York to be officially met by the Bishop o York who will bless him at York Minster.'

'Why not attack him there?'

Coleen answered 'There's an extra battalion o troops in place for his protection.'

Wath nodded and Liam continued.

173

'He's travelling up by train early Friday evening. The train will leave St Pancras at four-o clock and pass through here at seven. The first problem is the escort.'

'Escort?'

'Yes, they always send an engine ahead o the Royal train to clear any blockages so we cannot simply block the track.'

'How far ahead?'

'Normally the escort leads by half a mile.'

'So, if they are going through here at full speed, sixty miles an hour, that means a gap before the Royal train of thirty seconds.'

'Correct.'

'Not long enough to pull a rail loose.'

'Correct.'

'You need explosives.'

'What about the points?'

'The points on the main line have all been electrified. That means they are all controlled from the central signal box between Swinton and Mexborough. Any change, any tampering and they will know and it would take longer than thirty seconds for you to damage or over ride.'

'So how do we do it?'

'Right now, without explosives, I don't think you can. But go through the timings again. Will they be going at sixty miles an hour? Can we slow them down before they get here?'

Wath ran his finger along the MNER line lost in his thoughts.

'How many carriages on the escort?'

'Two.'

'How many on the Royal train?'

'Five.'

'There might be a way.'

Liam leant forward. Wath ignored him and looked at Coleen.

'It needs this lot' he threw a thumb over his shoulder at Patrick 'to follow instructions. Exactly. I can't be responsible for incompetents.' He heard shuffling behind him but a stare from Coleen stopped it.

'Tell us what to do.'

'When the train arrives here' he placed his finger on the map 'all the points on the MNER will be green from Rotherham almost through to Pontefract. At least five miles ahead of the train. Any problems and that gives them five minutes to slow down to a halt at a nice gentle pace. This will show on the control panel. But it also means that we have five minutes notice of the train arriving. When the signal goes green here' he pointed at the same spot on the map 'we know the train is five minutes away.'

'But we can't see the signal. It's too far away.' Liam was bright, seeing the problem immediately.

'True. But when that turns green on the MNER line the Wath Road Junction signal in that signal box' he pointed over his shoulder 'goes red to stop any traffic from the collieries or the GCR line going onto the MNER track.'

'Okay so we now know where the train is. How do we derail it?'

'Forget trying to drop it off the embankment at Low Common, that's not going to work. If you trace the colliery and GCR line back from the southern junction with the MNER it leads to Wath Hump. Loaded coal wagons are stored here ready for onward transit. It's called the hump because there is a hump. The wagons sit on top and when they are needed the brakes are released and gravity pulls them down.'

Wath halted tied up in his thoughts. Liam ran his finger down the track. He was quick, he had worked it out already.

'What about points?'

'It's a colliery line, it's not been electrified. The Government won't pay for it when it's about to give the pits back to the owners. It wants them to pay. So, all the points are controlled from that signal box by rod and pinion. Even better the MNER signal box has no idea what is happening up here. Once beyond their junction point it's just a void for them. They have to trust the men in that box.'

'How many points do the wagons go through?'

'This is the beauty. The colliery lines were built first and they were only concerned with getting their coal away. All the points are weighted or spring switches and apart from one they face in the right direction. Once a train in motion hits them the flange on the wheel forces the rails to open and they default one way, unless the signal box changes them, and the only one stopping a wagon going onto the MNER line is this one here.'

He pointed to the map. Liam bent over the table and followed the line down making marks at each break in the line and each signal point. After a few minutes he looked back up.

'Okay. So how do we get past that?'

'Every point has a lever at its side to enable it to be manually switched.'

'So, we throw the switch.'

'Not quite. There are no services planned on the colliery or GCR tracks between twenty to and ten past seven so the points will be set to default. Fifteen minutes before the train is due one of you lot goes down to that set of points with metal cutters. Once you've cut the rod connecting that point to the signal box then you manually change the signal over. With the rod cut the signal won't move and the signal box will not know what has happened and won't be able to change it back.'

'Why don't we just take control o the signal box and change the signal from there rather than cutting it?'

'You'll need control of the box later but all the signals will be showing stop meaning they will all be facing down. If you cut the rod all the signal arms will still be down. If you change that signal from inside the box, one of them will change, become horizontal. It only takes one railway man to look, to see a wrong signal and they will know. And believe me with the Royal train coming through they will be looking. Then it only takes them five seconds to throw a switch and everything is over.'

'Okay we cut the signal, so now the line is clear from Wath Hump all the way onto the MNER line.'

'That's right and you have five minutes notice of the train approaching. It should be quiet in the Hump at that time of night so you go in and release the brakes on a couple of wagons and let them run down the line. Because its downhill all the way they should take less than four minutes to get to the MNER line. Now it's just a matter of timing. Of making sure that the escort has passed and the wagons run into the gap between the trains. Once they are in that gap on the MNER line the Royal train can't avoid them. Loaded the wagons weigh twenty tons each and will be doing at least forty miles an hour, the train sixty in the opposite direction. It's a disaster.'

The room was quiet as Liam poured over the map. Coleen looked at Wath with a satisfied smile on her face. Patrick and the other two men were leant against the wall absorbed in the conversation at the table. Liam looked up.

'How do we know when to release the wagons? The men on the brakes won't be able to see what's going off.'

'That's when you need control of the signal box. You will see the Wath Junction signal change. Know exactly where the escort is. When the timings are right you change the signal inside Wath Central Station, that's the sixth handle in from the left-hand side. The men at the hump will be able to see that but not the men in the Swinton and Mexborough box and it will not affect the line to the MNER. That's the signal to release the wagons.'

'What about the timings?'

'That's your department. There's a thirty second window between the escort and the Royal train. That's the window you have to hit. Release too early and the escort will take the punishment meaning the Royal train will be able to slow down to a crawl. It may still derail but it might not. Release the wagons after the window, missing the gap, and it will be gone.'

Coleen leant across the table 'What do you think Liam?'

'I think it's perfect. We'll be nearly a mile and a half from the action. We don't need explosives all we need is gravity. The timings need to be spot on' he looked at Wath 'will you check me on that?'

'I've done my bit. If it screws up now it's down to you lot. I want no more involvement. That was the deal.'

'How do I know how fast the wagons drop from the hump?'

'You watch and time. Pretend to be a train spotter. You look the part.'

Every head turned to Coleen. She looked at the youngest person in the room. 'Can you do it Liam?'

'That I can, but a check would be nice.'

'I'll check it. Pretty boy has done what we asked' she turned to Wath 'but you keep your fecking mouth shut.'

Wath nodded.

Chapter Twenty Nine

Tuesday 20/4/1920

After an uncomfortable night Wath checked the oil and water on the lorry and started the engine but before he could reverse out of the yard Patrick appeared at his side with another man.

'This is Billy' he said 'Coleen thought you might want a bit o company today.'

Wath looked at the man then at Patrick. 'I'm not to be trusted then?'

'Let's just say it's for yer own peace o mind.'

There was no point arguing. If he did, they would assume he was going to talk to the authorities. Best just get on with it. 'Climb in' he said to Billy then to Patrick 'he'd better be a good worker cos he ain't just sitting there having a ride.'

'He'll do what you ask' Patrick leant towards him smirking 'relax, consider it help, cos he'll be with you all week.'

Wath pulled out of the yard and started the day. His first delivery was a load of coke from Manvers to Adwick Foundry then onto West Field Farm for sand. He looked across at Billy. There was a dour looking man if he had ever seen one. Wath idly wondered when was the last time he had smiled or laughed. It was going to be a long day and an even longer week.

Thursday 22/4/1920

Coleen lifted her head from the map and the list of timings written on the side.

'Okay I agree. The timings work. We check out the wagons in the stock yard an hour before and find the four we want to release. They must be linked, fully loaded and on the down slope. Patrick cuts the rod to the signal at a quarter to seven. At the same time the men, all four o them, go to the hump. If they meet any resistance, they take care o it. Quietly.

'When Patrick gets back, we three go into the signal box at five to. Once the flag changes we wait for one minute and ten seconds then send the signal. The men release the brakes on the four wagons. There is only a twenty second gap to get them moving. They jog after the wagons, when they get back, we take the lorry and drive to Barnsley where we catch the LYR service and are away.'

'We don't stay for the show?'

'No. There's nothing to see anyway.'

'I know, I've been thinking about that. Why don't we set fire to the wagons? It would be spectacular then. Flaming wagons derailing the Royal train.'

'How do we do that?'

'Each man takes a jerry can o petrol into the yard, climbs up and pours it over the coal in the wagon. As they come past here, we throw petrol bombs on them and whoosh we've got a fireball heading down the track at forty miles an hour.'

'What do you think Patrick?'

'Better than just runaway wagons. Imagine the headlines in the papers. Everybody will know we did it.'

'Okay get the petrol.'

'What do we do about the Englishman?' Liam scrutinised Coleen.

'He did his bit. I gave my word.'

'Coleen I'm with Patrick on this, he's not to be trusted.'

'So, what do you propose?'

'We take him to one side and dispose o him.'

'He'll be missed.'

'By who?'

'The one-armed neighbour. They go to the pub every Friday at six o clock it's a religion.'

'So, we dispose o him too.'

180

'How? The signal box sees everything that happens in this yard. They would know.'

'But what can they do?'

'Ever heard o morse code? They have a bell signal between boxes - he could alert others.'

'We should take over the signal box earlier.'

'Then how do we know what to do if a bell rings or a flag changes?'

'So, what do we do?'

'We watch him. Look we need his lorry. Let him go to the pub with his neighbour. That way the only person who sees what is happening is the signalman. We send somebody to watch him at the pub. They can stand outside. If anything looks suspicious, they go inside and challenge him. He'll not risk us hurting his girlfriends. No wait, I'll go to the pub. I'll watch him.'

Patrick listened to the discussion. 'We should kill him, Coleen.'

'No, it's riskier than trusting him. But you know I'll do what's necessary if needed.'

'Why not do both? You inside the pub and a man outside.'

'That's good.'

Patrick watched as Liam started to nod his head slowly. They were both more comfortable now that Coleen was watching him. They knew she would do whatever was needed.

'Okay but we need you back before the action starts.'

'I'll wait until twenty minutes before seven and we'll both come back. Pretty boy won't have time to do anything then.'

'What do we do about the signalman?'

'Tie him up and blindfold him. Any trouble you do what you have to do.'

Liam and Patrick looked at Coleen. She nodded 'We know what we're doing. Let's get packed and make everything ready to throw onto the lorry. But do it out o sight o the signalman.'

'What if he doesn't come back with the lorry?'

'He will, remember Billy is with him.'

Chapter Thirty

It was the first time he had seen Henry's car parked at Twentieth Century Concrete. It was also the first time he had been asked to deliver cement. This was outside the contract and a special request from Henry. As he pulled into the loading bay George strutted over 'Henry wants to see you, instructions for the delivery. We'll load it. He's inside.'

Billy was the far side of the lorry, unable to hear the conversation, he marched around and grabbed Wath 'What's happening?'

'It's the first time I've delivered cement for them, they want to give me instructions. Just help them with the loading and keep your mouth shut.'

'He' Billy pointed at George 'looked as if he could kill you.'

'Aye there's history, he don't like me and I don't like him. Forget it, just don't cause a fuss.'

He walked inside where Henry was sat behind his desk. He motioned for Wath to sit in the chair opposite, lit a cigarette and threw the packet across the table. Wath picked them up 'Marlborough. Sophisticated.'

Henry frowned 'That's Lucy talking.'

Wath nodded in acknowledgement, pleased to have annoyed Henry, took a cigarette, lit it and tossed the packet back onto the table 'So, what's the special instructions?'

'Don't break the bags.'

'That's it.'

'That's it. I just wanted a talk.'

Wath looked at him intrigued: they had nothing to talk about. 'What's going off?'

'Eh?' Wath's heart missed a beat. Did he know about him and Lucy?

'What's going off with Coleen?'

Wath relaxed, this was safer ground 'No idea. Says she'll be going back to Dublin in a couple of days.'

'She's the biggest liar I've ever met and that includes you.'

'I'll try to find a compliment in there somewhere.'

'What's going off Dyson? I've paid her for the farm, she has the money, why is she still here?'

'Told you I don't know.'

'Look' Henry leant across the table and pointed at Wath 'I know how much money there is in carting. I could have my own lorries moving the sand from the farm to here but I don't. Why? Because there's not enough money in it. So, I know there's not enough money for you to pay a hired hand and that hired hand is one of Coleen's men. Let me ask again, what's going off?'

'He's bored just wants to help.'

'Bollocks. She's put a guard on you… she's put a guard on you because you know something.'

Wath stared at Henry trying not to move a muscle in his face. Henry glared at him tapping the packet of cigarettes on the shiny desk top. Several seconds passed. Eventually Henry said 'That woman is evil. She's up to something.'

'So why did you do business with her.'

'Didn't have much choice.'

'Not what I heard. You went looking for her, made her an offer on the farm.'

'What. What has that bitch told you?'

'She's told me about that day when the four of you went to the farm and assaulted her. Though she admits you walked away. Edwin came back and attacked the other three. She went into hiding in Manchester where you chased her down and made her an offer to rent the farm.'

Henry was staring at Wath with a look of complete disbelief on his face. 'That fucking lying bitch.' He stood up and walked to a cabinet, pulled two glasses and a bottle of whiskey from a shelf. Pouring a large shot into each of the glasses he pushed one towards Wath then drained his. Wath left the second glass where it was.

'You need to know what you are dealing with.' He placed the empty glass on the table and tapped it in agitation 'No one attacked Coleen.'

He looked at Wath, hesitating. His expression torn between anger and frustration all coated in a thick veneer of disbelief. 'No one attacked Coleen' he repeated almost to himself 'when we realised Edwin was out in the fields I didn't walk away - I was sent to fetch him. As we came back to the farm, she ran out of the farmhouse covered in blood.

'She attacked them!'

His eyes were staring into space looking back over the years, the decades, into the day of the murders.

'She killed them. Murdered them, there and then. All three of them. We went into the house… it was like a slaughter house gone mad. There was blood everywhere. I was young, sacred stiff. Edwin made me promise not to say a word. Said they would let me have the farm if I kept quiet. He took the blame because she was pregnant. That's right he took the blame cos she was pregnant, then she left you on that gravestone. Bitch.'

Henry lifted his head and stared into Wath's face.

'Edwin was a good man.'

He was breathing heavily, the tension of his words cramping his lungs, draining them of oxygen. He sucked in air in a huge gasp and continued.

'Once he'd been hung, she contacted me, agreed to rent me the farm - which was not what Edwin promised but it was too late. I couldn't say anything. I'd let an innocent man go to the gallows. Now she's back with my money in her pocket and she is definitely up to something.'

184

He poured himself another drink and emptied the glass. A mild sweat broke out on his forehead. He sat dejected and lit another cigarette blowing the smoke at the ceiling. Wath sat unmoving not saying a word.

'What's she up to?'

'I've told you I don't know.'

'And I don't believe you.'

'That's your problem' Wath stood up 'I'll not break any bags. Thanks for the fag.' He turned and left. His drink untouched.

Climbing into the cab he sat with his head in his hands until Billy and the men had loaded all the bags. Finished Billy started to climb in alongside him but before he had the chance to sit in the passenger seat Wath launched at him 'Did they ask you anything? What did you say?'

'Nothin.'

'Nothing?'

'Nothin.'

'You're a liar.' Wath pushed the lorry into gear and started to drive ignoring the pained expression on Billy's face. The cement was due to be delivered to West Melton as part of the concrete house experiment. Instead Wath turned down Common Lane and drove into Treacle Town. Slamming the brakes on he jumped out before Billy could say a word and stormed into the Jenkinson's. There were several men crowded around a map along with Liam, Patrick and Coleen.

'Get them out, we need to talk. Just me, you and Patrick.'

Coleen and Patrick looked at each other. Coleen said 'It's alright boys just give us a minute please.'

The men filed out, all eyeballing Wath with venom. He stood by the door until they had all left then slammed it shut. 'What the fuck is going off' he yelled 'did you set up Henry to test me?'

'Whoa pretty boy, calm down. What're you on about… Henry?'

'I got called into Twentieth Century today. Henry wanted to see me. He quizzes me about you, I say nothing then he says he knows

185

Billy is a minder. He knows because he knows I can't afford hired hands. Did you set it up, was that a test?'

Coleen raised her hands palm out above her shoulders in a "no way" gesture. 'Nothing was set up. Tell me what he said.'

'I just told you. I said Billy was bored and just helping out, a volunteer, but Patrick you need to ask him what he said to Henry's men while I was in with Henry. He won't tell me.'

Coleen nodded to Patrick 'Go ask him Patrick.'

Patrick left as Wath sat down at the table still boiling with rage.

'We didn't set that up pretty boy. What else did he say?'

'He said that Edwin didn't kill those men. He said you did.'

'Ahh… so now you think I'm a murderer and a liar.'

'I don't know what to think.'

'Well, you'll just have to decide who to believe won't you?'

'That's it. You aren't going to challenge or deny?'

'What good would it do. You've heard my story. Believe it or believe Henry. The choice is yours.' They stared at each other as Patrick re-entered.

'He screwed it. He told the men loading the wagon, someone called George, that he was the new hired hand.'

'Oh shit. That's Henry's brother.'

Coleen and Patrick looked hard at each other.

'It's no worry Patrick. They won't understand what's happening in time.'

Wath slammed his fists against the table 'Great. What about me. I've got to stay here once you're gone.'

'You'll find a way to talk your way out o it.'

'Jesus Coleen you're one hard bitch.'

'One hard bitch who got you a lorry and got you to see your daughter don't forget.'

He nodded. This was one way traffic. He couldn't believe a word either of them said and couldn't trust them as far as he could throw them left-handed. She was a liar Patrick was a liar and Henry was a liar. His only conciliation was that he was a liar too.

186

Nevertheless, he would keep his word but only if she kept hers. Only if Lucy and Betty were safe.

He needed to get away from them and think.

'Look I have a delivery to make otherwise it will be even more suspicious. Billy will have to come with me but he keeps his mouth shut. Just one word from him and I'll break all his teeth.'

'I'll speak to him.' Patrick left once more.

'Coleen, I can't help you anymore. I'm not good in a team, I can't handle incompetents. I've kept my word. I want you to keep yours. Lucy and Betty go unharmed and I am away from here when this happens.'

'Where will you be?'

'In the Nelson where everyone can see me.'

'You know my word, it's good, they won't be hurt. Go make your delivery.'

Wath drove out of the yard with Billy sat po faced at his side. They did not talk. While they made the delivery Wath sat in the cab and watched Billy do all the work. He was drenched in sweat and covered in cement powder when he sat back in the cab. Still not a word passed between them as Wath drove back. As he slowed to manoeuvre through the junction in the middle of town a voice cried 'Wath. Wait.' He turned and looked at the pavement, Lucy was stood waving with Alice alongside. He pulled in to the side, looked at Billy and spat 'That's my daughter. You wait here.'

He climbed out and walked over. Lucy was full of smiles.

'Hi, I just thought we might organise another… you know… meeting… this weekend.' There was an undertone to her voice. A promise.

'That would be great, same time, same place' he smiled at Alice 'don't forget the apples.'

Lucy gave him a strange look 'Are you ok?'

He turned his back on Alice 'Few problems. Listen do me a favour tell Henry he was right. I was lying.'

'What!'

187

'I was lying. Tell him to load his gun, lock the door and not to let anyone in tonight.

'Wath, what are you on about? You're scaring me.'

'Good. Tell Henry.'

'Wath!'

'See you later.'

He walked back to the lorry aware of Lucy's stare beating into the back of his head. Ignoring the feeling he climbed in and faced Billy 'Before you ask that was me failing to arrange seeing my daughter at the weekend. Put that in your report.' He grabbed the wheel and pulled back onto the road.

Chapter Thirty One

Friday 23/4/1920

The taxi was waiting as Smedley banged on Goulding's door. The big man answered and looked down at him.

'Get your uniform on we're going to Barnsley.'

'Eh, what, why?'

'Somebody has booked seven tickets on the eight-o clock service from Barnsley to Liverpool, then they've booked overnight on the LYR shipping company from Liverpool to Drogheda. But here's the kicker they paid using a five-pound note from the robbery. We need to get to Barnsley and get the locals on board. Me and you can't arrest seven men at once. But when the Barnsley lads have got them, we question them.'

'Can't the Barnsley lads handle it?'

'I think they might be your Irishmen from Treacle Town. You know them, you will recognise them and make arresting them easier and, if he did do the robbery, I reckon Dyson will be with them. Come on we've not got all night.'

Goulding grinned as he grabbed his uniform jacket.

Wath knocked on Jimmy's door 'Come on mate' he yelled.

'Minute' Jimmy replied.

Wath stood waiting, watching the Irishman sat on the step of the end terrace. His hackles were up but there was nothing he could do. Coleen had made it clear that she would attack Lucy or Betty unless he kept quiet.

The Royal train, Prince Albert. There would be hell to play. He had spent three years in the trenches fighting for King and Country and had nothing but a deep dislike of the nobility who formed the core of the officer ranks. Some of them were exceptionally brave, walking into battle with little more than a swagger stick and a pistol, but most were arrogant, self-centred egoists who had servants to do their dirty work then drank wine and ate steak while the men suffered in the mud. Inside the rigid class system in the United Kingdom, they were the next layer down from the royals. He could not imagine how pampered Prince Albert, the future king, was.

But Wath had fought for his country and no matter how he tried to justify it to himself this was an attack on his country. The Irish had rebelled at the height of the build up to the fighting on the Somme hoping that the weakened forces in Ireland would be over whelmed. They were wrong. Coleen's husband had been part of the Easter Rising and had paid the penalty, now she was seeking revenge and she had used him. He felt dirty, infected but powerless.

He needed to get to the Nelson and have a drink. He needed to be away from Treacle Town when it happened.

Jimmy finally emerged, Wath was so engrossed in his thoughts he did not even register Frank waving from the signal box. They walked up Common Lane turning into Edna Street without Wath speaking a word. Walking up Winifred Road they could see a man stood opposite the pub entrance. It was one of the Irishmen. He was stood leant against the wall watching the pub intently. Wath grimaced. They obviously did not trust him.

On entering the pub, a smiling Betty greeted them pulling their pints. They moved to their usual table where the domino team acknowledged them.

'You alright?' Jimmy asked 'you've been awful quiet.'

'Aye just got a lot on my mind at the moment.'

As he said it Coleen walked in, ordered a drink and sat between Wath and the domino table. 'Hello boys' she said in a cheerful voice.

Jimmy smiled and raised his glass in greeting. Wath ignored her.

'Cat got your tongue pretty boy?'

Wath stared at her, unable to think of anything to say he shrugged and took a drink from his glass. Jimmy took it upon himself to speak into the silence.

'So, Coleen, are you settling in, getting used to Treacle Town?'

'Got to say it's a hard place to get comfortable in but not be long now. Back to Dublin soon.' She watched the dominoes shaking her head as Tom played.

'You've come at the wrong time' Jimmy opined 'it's busier than normal, pits are moving more coal out before the Government passes them back to the owners. Get as much money as they can.'

'What'll happen then?' asked Coleen.

Wath groaned. That was all Jimmy needed to go on a long passionate speech about Nationalisation, private owners, unions and strikes. As Jimmy climbed onto his soap box Wath signalled he was getting the drinks and moved to the bar. Passing their drinks over he went back to the bar and stood talking to Betty.

Every time the door opened, he looked out and could see the Irishman stood leaning against the wall opposite. As usual on a Friday night Betty was kept busy by the pace of drinking so he leant against the bar embracing his pint with half an ear to Jimmy's diatribe.

He looked around the pub.

Normality reigned.

The dominoes were in full swing, the young lads had been joined by another of their mates and were deep in discussion about football while all the other regulars were sat at their tables enjoying Friday night.

No one realised the anomaly: the Irishman outside.

He sipped his beer watching Betty pull another pint. Could he have done anything to stop the Irish? Refusing to help would have resulted in a prison sentence of that he was sure and he was determined never to go to prison again. He could live with what he had said. The youngster Liam was bright and would have worked out the way to derail the train, he just got him there quicker. But now he had to sit and watch otherwise they would take it out on Lucy or Betty or possibly both.

He had warned Lucy, she would be at home behind a locked door with Henry's loaded shotgun for protection. Betty was in front of him where he could watch and protect. He had done all he could but the Irishman outside and Coleen inside the pub rattled him.

Suddenly he realised Coleen was at his side. She placed her hand on his shoulder. He winced but left it there.

'I'm going now. Been good knowing you pretty boy, look after yourself.'

'Bye.'

She looked him up and down, smiled, nodded her head and turned. As she walked through the doors, he saw the Irishman leave the wall and walk across the road to join her. He picked up his pint and moved back to Jimmy.

'Jesus Wath you're poor company tonight. What's got into yer?'

'Lots on my mind' he watched the clock on the wall move to quarter to seven. It seemed to crawl. He imagined Patrick cutting the rod to the signal and the other men entering the Hump.

The Royal train and he was just sat here like Coleen's stooge.

The clock ticked around moving past ten to.

He put his beer down. His chest was throbbing he couldn't just sit here. He had to do something. He turned to Jimmy.

'Just nipping out, be back in a minute. Will you do me a favour?'

'What's that?'

'Watch Betty. Don't let anything happen to her.'

Jimmy stared at him. 'What's going off?'

The clock clicked to five to.

'Nothing I can't handle, back in a minute.'

He stood up and moved through the interior doors into the porch. When the doors had closed behind him, he reached up and grabbed the pick axe handle from its hiding place then started to jog down Winifred Road.

There was no sign of Coleen or the Irishman but rather than cross over to Common Lane he followed Winifred Road staying out of sight of the signal box. At the bottom of the road, he turned past the pig sty and jumped the fence onto the track.

Fifty yards away the signal arm was down as it should be.

He looked up the line to the signal box.

He could see Coleen, Patrick and Liam inside. They were all looking the other way towards the Hump. He placed his hand on the track, there was the faintest of tremors where there should have been nothing.

The wagons were starting to move.

Holding his handle at the ready in case anyone was protecting the points he moved towards the signal. The tremor was now stronger. He could hear it, there was no need to feel the track. The wagons were picking up speed, building momentum.

He reached the points and grabbed the manual handle. It was limp. Patrick had cut its rods too.

There was no way to switch the points.

He could see the wagons now. A dark mass trundling down the track. He ran to the end of the switch rail where it touched the main rail. He looked around for something to wedge the rails open. The only thing he could see was a cobble of coal. He rammed his handle into the rails and levered the rails apart pushing the cobble in between.

He could hear the wheels of the wagons as they moved over the rails. They were gaining pace the ker clunks were coming faster, less time in between.

He released the pick axe handle ready to jump to the side but as he did the rails crushed the cobble and sprang back into position.

Suddenly everything lit up with a whoosh.

He looked up the track. The wagons were on fire.

Standing on the track, even without the extra light, he was as exposed as if stranded in No Man's Land. There was nowhere to hide and he could see faces in the signal box looking at him.

193

Then arms pointing at him.

The flaming wagons were almost on him travelling at over twenty miles an hour. Still gaining speed. He grabbed his handle and pushed it in between the rails again.

He levered them open, just an inch.

Would it be enough?

He held the handle in place and leant back as far as he could, as far back from the wagons as possible, desperate to be out of the way while still levering the rails, holding the gap open.

The wagons were on him.

He heard the crack of a pistol as someone shot at him from the signal box. They were too far away for that to have any effect.

Then the wagons were between them. Hiding him from the signal box.

Still, he held the gap open as the wagons hit the points. The front wheel passed the switch and hit the handle breaking it in two. The momentum threw him down the line, spinning him around. His head and shoulder smashed into the wagon. It hit him at twenty miles an hour cartwheeling him backwards away from the track.

Wath crashed to the ground skidding across the ballast at the side. But he had seen the wheel go past the point taking the switch rail – he had done it.

But it was only one wheel.

The far wheel remained on the main rail. All the following wheels stayed on the main rail.

One wheel.

Just one wheel off.

The wagon screeched then shuddered and bounced as the wheel fought to stay on the switch rail while the other wheels fought to stay on the main rail. The momentum forced the wheel off the switch track. It jumped up, left the track and fell back down battering into a wooden sleeper. Once again it leapt into the air. If it came back down on the main rail his efforts would be for nothing.

It didn't.

It missed the rail crashing into the next sleeper, crushing the sleeper, before it dug into the gravel throwing up dust and stones. It hit the sleeper behind burying itself in the gravel and stayed there.

The back of the wagon rose as it tried to push past the obstacle. The next wagon crashed into it and flaming coal leapt into the air. The wagons twisted, carried by their momentum.

They lurched and started to fall.

The burning coals thrown up from the initial impact rained down on Wath, he curled into the foetal position and covered his head with his arms.

The cobbles thudded into him.

The wagons continued to twist, jack knifing off the rails and into the air. They left the track then fell away from him crashing into the buildings on the far side of the track. The Jenkinson's took the brunt of the collision but the next three terraces all had wagons smash into them. The blazing hot coals fell out of the wagons into the houses, crashing through into the cellars. The top floors wobbled and swayed then came down with a thump.

The bricks fell across the yard. Slates and roof tiles followed.

They fell onto the lorry burying the rear in a cloud of dust.

The impact continued to vibrate through the houses and badly built as they were and weakened by years of vibrations from passing trains they shook, then collapsed until there was just one wall left standing. The end wall to the terrace.

Wath watched as Treacle Town disappeared in a cloud of dust and flames then he slipped into unconsciousness.

Frank was blindfolded and tied up in the corner. Coleen watched the wagons start to move. No flags had changed, all was under control. The switch points had been cut, the signal changed inside Wath Central Station at exactly the right time and now the wagons were moving. Patrick and Liam stood at the top of the steps outside, petrol bombs at their feet.

She could feel the excitement racing through her body.

The wagons were gaining speed. She could hear them, feel them on the track. Patrick and Liam picked up the milk bottles full of petrol with the burning rag stuffed inside. Patrick threw first then Liam, then Patrick again. Suddenly the whole sky lit up as the bottles smashed and the petrol burst into flames. She closed her eyes from the glare. Then quickly opened them. She could not miss this.

It was spectacular.

She moved to get a better view looking down the railway line towards Manvers and Mexborough. Towards the collision zone. There was a figure stood alongside the track. The glare from the wagons lit him up as he tried to change the switch rail. Patrick was by her side. He saw the figure and yelled, grabbing a pistol from his pocket. He leant out of the window and shot but the wagons were in between.

Suddenly the wagons bucked.

The first dug its nose into the ground and the rest hit it. Twisting and turning, throwing flaming coals into the air, the wagons reared and started to cartwheel. They left the track, jumping into the air, somersaulting into the terrace.

The signal box shook as the wagons hit the brickwork of the terrace. The houses seemed to implode then fall crazily into the yard. The coals tumbled from the wagons pouring into the front rooms and cellars of the houses. Flames from the petrol doused cobbles leapt into the air.

Liam had been right the burning wagons turned the whole thing into a breath-taking drama. But the drama was being played out in Treacle Town and not with the Royal train. The men had returned from the Hump and were stood at the bottom of the steps watching the inferno blaze while she, Patrick and Liam watched it from the height of the signal box. Their possessions were burning in the firestorm that had been the Jenkinson's house. Their means of escape, the lorry, was covered in bricks and slate. It would be impossible to move the vehicle and the flames from the fire were licking ever closer. She stood and watched.

It was a disaster.

She heard someone talking to her 'Coleen we need to leave.'

Looking at Liam she stopped her introspection and started to think. They needed to get away. The tickets for the train in Barnsley were useless. Now the lorry was out of commission they would never get there in time. She grabbed her bag and led them down the steps to join the men. At the bottom she dug inside and pulled out the sack holding the money from the robbery. She counted roughly two hundred pounds from the sack then passed the remainder over to Liam.

'There's around five hundred pounds there. You take the men that way' she pointed away from Wath upon Dearne towards Bolton and Thurnscoe 'give them one hundred pounds each and split up. All o you find your own way back to Dublin. There's more than enough money there to do it. But split up. They'll be looking for a gang. Go your own way. Do your own thing. I'll see you back in Dublin.'

'What about the Englishman? What are you going to do?'

'I made a promise to him. I intend to keep it.' Liam nodded and led the men away. She closed her bag and turned towards Common Lane 'Come on Patrick we've work to do.'

In the distance she could hear ringing bells getting closer as fire engines from the two collieries approached. Looking up Common Lane she could see men running down, heading for the fire. She changed her mind, there were too many people coming down the road 'This way Patrick' she called and turned onto the railway line walking away from the inferno towards Wath Central Station.

They marched in silence for over two hundred yards. Then as they approached the Station, they left the railway and walked up Station Road.

'What're we doing Coleen? Your Englishman is buried under tonnes o burning coal.'

'Yeah, but I need to put one o his girls out o action. Just in case he survives.'

197

'We need to get away from here.'

'Patrick, I intend to carry out my threat. I made him a promise – his girl dies. But there's a bonus. Henry has a car. We'll take that and put some miles between us before we get onto a train.'

Patrick nodded. 'I like it.'

They both smiled grimly and strode on up High Street heading for Fitzwilliam Street.

Chapter Thirty Two

Friday 23/4/1920

He could smell burning.

His head hurt and his body ached from top to bottom.

Wath slowly regained consciousness. He pulled his hands from his head they were covered in blood. There were lights spinning in front of his eyes. He twisted and vomited hard onto the embankment. He was covered in coal, some of which was ablaze. He moved left and right, shaking himself clear of the rubble on him. Pushing himself onto his knees he realised his coat was burning, smouldering. He patted it down. There was a burn on his arm and one on his leg. He rubbed his head and felt the blood oozing from a cut above his right ear.

Staggering to his feet he looked across the railway line. Treacle Town was trashed. Only one wall remained standing. There were fires in the houses closest to the signal box while the yard was full of mounds of brick and timber and dust.

His lorry was covered in detritus.

Lurching forward he stumbled towards the mess. He had saved the Royal train and destroyed Treacle Town. An equation most would see balanced in the right direction.

Not him.

Not Jimmy.

The flames were leaping towards the signal box and suddenly he remembered Frank. Swaying as he tried to speed up, he staggered past the box and climbed the steps. Frank was laid at the far side of the room. His feet and hands were tied and there was a blindfold around his eyes. Wath floundered as he reeled from side to side, crashing into the panel. He reached Frank and ripped the blindfold off. Frank stared at him panic written all over his face.

Smoke poured in through the open window.

Flames lapped the side of the signal box.

Wath could feel the heat.

There was no time for ceremony. He grabbed Frank and threw him over his shoulder. The fifteen feet to the door felt like a marathon. He battered it open and stumbled down the steps. Twenty paces later he could do no more and collapsed at the side of the railway crossing. Frank rolled onto his back as Wath sat grabbing air, sucking it through the smoke, sweat pouring from him as blood ran down his face and neck from the wound above his ear.

He looked at Frank as he lay there. Hands and feet tied.

'Took your time coming back, dint you.' Frank said stone faced, then smiled and burst out laughing. They both tried to laugh but ended up coughing and spluttering as the smoke took effect. This only made the laughing worse and as the colliery fire engine screamed to a halt at the side of them, they were laid on the floor gibbering like a couple of demented idiots.

A crowd gathered by the crossing watching the fire and the attempts of the two fire engines to put it out, the men were well trained and knew their job. It was a matter of minutes before the fire was under control and only burning in two of the cellars. Manvers Main ambulance had followed the fire engines and the pit ambulance man inspected Frank and Wath.

Frank, he announced was fine but Wath needed stitches and treatment for several burns. He wiped the blood away from the head wound and covered it in antiseptic cream as a temporary measure.

Wath's head was spinning.

He turned away from the fire scanning the crowd watching from the crossing, he could see Walt and Jack. Bill and Syd were stood behind them with Jimmy and Betty. She was crying but she was safe. Jimmy had his arm around her.

The scene in front of him rolled then twisted, he vomited again. The Ambulance man looked at him with more concern.

'You're concussed. Let's get you out of here.'

He helped Wath to his feet. He let the man support him, looking once again at the crowd trying to give a smile of assurance. As he did a car pulled in behind the crowd and Lucy and Henry got out. Wath stopped the ambulanceman and peered through the onlookers. Pushing the ambulanceman away he staggered towards the crossing. Lucy raced from the car, threw herself on him and grabbed him in a bear hug. Henry watched stern faced from the back of the crowd. Betty turned her head into Jimmy's shoulder.

'Thank God you're alright.'

Suddenly a realisation hit Wath as hard as the runaway wagons had. Alice! Coleen had said females. Her words echoed inside his head "it won't be you I'll be leaving on the gravestone next time but one of your females." And then she had promised not to hurt Lucy or Betty – by name. He had assumed she meant Lucy or Betty but there was a third – Alice.

He ignored Lucy's concern 'Where's Alice?' he asked bluntly.

'At home.' Lucy replied. Shocked at his attitude.

'Who with?'

'Mum. Why?'

'I told you to stay at home. I told you to lock the door.'

'Yeah' Henry had joined them and interrupted 'we've come down to find out why, to find out what's happening.'

'Jesus Henry. I warned you. Coleen's threatened to harm someone important to me. Get back in the car. Get us back to your house. I need to know Alice is safe.'

Lucy and Henry stared open mouthed at Wath. They seemed incapable of taking in what was happening.

Wath made the decision for them, lurching past them towards the car and virtually falling into the back seat. It had the desired effect. They jumped into the car. Henry started the motor as Lucy turned around in the passenger seat.

'You look awful, are you ok?'

'Fine.'

'What happened?'

'Coleen and her Irishmen were here to attack the Royal train. They were going to derail it. I derailed their runaway wagons early. She'll be looking for revenge.'

'Where is she?'

'I don't know but I want to know Alice is safe.'

'I told you she was the devil!' Henry threw over his shoulder.

'Yeah, and I told you to stay in with the door locked and your shotgun loaded.'

'Stop it! This is no time for arguing. Henry get us home.'

They all sat in silence as Henry drove like a mad man, tearing through the streets. The house gates were still open and he screamed in, gravel spitting everywhere as he hit the brakes. He and Lucy jumped out racing into the house. Wath followed more carefully his aching limbs starting to seize. He followed them through the open door and stood in the hallway. He heard Lucy scream 'Mother.' Henry raced past him up the stairs yelling 'Alice, Alice.'

He followed Lucy's sobs into the kitchen. An elderly woman was sat on the floor crying with an obviously broken nose streaming blood. Lucy held a towel to her. 'What happened Mam?'

'A man and a woman came in asking for you' The woman sobbed, the sound choked as blood ran from her nose 'when I said you were out, they hit me and then pulled Alice outside. I don't understand - she said she was Alice's grandma.'

Wath had heard enough. Henry was still running around upstairs shouting Alice, Lucy was in floods of tears trying to stop her mother bleeding.

Coleen had taken Alice.

There was only one place she was going, the gravestone.

She was going back to Abel's stone, back to where she had left him to die.

He limped back through the house out of the door, across Stump Cross Road and down Chapel Street pushing his body to move as fast as it could. He could hear Alice shouting. The field at the far side of the road was empty and the leafy drives nearside hid the stone-built houses. The road was deserted.

Where were the good people of Wath upon Dearne?

The light was just beginning to fade as half way down the road he saw two figures turn past the Methodist Chapel onto Church Street. He was sure the larger figure had something over his shoulder. Golden locks cascading down his back.

He pushed harder. The distance closed and he was only twenty yards behind as they entered the churchyard heading towards the bell tower and the path to Abel's grave. He knew Patrick had a pistol, he had nothing. He followed scanning the ground looking for a weapon. There were flowers on a grave, he grabbed the vase. It was made from stone he threw the flowers onto the floor.

'Hello Patrick' he called.

Patrick stopped and dropped the bundle he was carrying. He turned thrusting his hand into his pocket pulling out a pistol. Coleen grabbed a screaming Alice by the hand and dragged her away. Wath moved so that the grave stone hid his right hand from Patrick.

'I knew we couldn't trust you' panted Patrick, his exertions carrying a squirming, fighting Alice for three hundred yards had winded him.

He pulled the pistol up to chest height and aimed at Wath. Wath feigned to move left then pushed off to the right throwing the vase with all the speed he could manage. Patrick pulled the trigger and a bullet hit the grave stone spitting splinters into Wath's face. He leapt forward following the vase which thudded into Patrick chest causing him to stagger backwards. Throwing himself at Patrick, he grabbed him before he could recover. They both fell to the floor, Wath on top. As they hit the floor the jolt caused Patrick to fire the pistol. A wild uncontrolled shot, the bullet flying into the canopy of the trees above.

Patrick was quick and strong. He was a fighter.

But there was fighting and fighting for your life and Wath only knew one way to fight. Patrick bucked and reared trying to move Wath to one side to bring the pistol to bear.

Wath let him lift him, then as Patrick started to move his weight to turn the gun, Wath collapsed dropping all his weight onto Patrick, concentrating on landing right elbow first. The pointed bone bore down hitting Patrick in the left eye. Wath's weight followed and he felt the eye pop as it burst and the bone around splintered. Patrick screamed, his grip on the pistol relaxed and Wath grabbed for it.

Pushing it into Patrick's stomach he pulled the trigger and Patrick screamed again.

Wath had seen many men gut shot, none of them survived, but all of them died a slow lingering death. He pulled himself from Patrick and stood up. Swaying groggily over the crying man he aimed the pistol and shot him through the chest.

The crying stopped.

Wearily he shuffled past the body and around the bell tower. Coleen was stood by Abel's grave, Alice held in front of her, a knife across her throat. He pointed the pistol at Coleen.

'It's over Coleen, let her go.'

Coleen scowled at him, her face pulled tight, the veins on her neck throbbing.

'I promised if you broke your word.'

'I never promised not to interfere Coleen. Let her go.'

'I—'

'— Coleen if you want to leave, let her go, otherwise I'll kill you.'

'I can't trust you.'

'Let her go.' In the distance he could hear Lucy shouting, screaming Alice's name.

'Put the gun down.'

'What?'

'Put the gun down then I'll let her go.'

'How can I trust you?'

'Put the gun down. Stand still and I walk away. She goes free.'

Wath knew he could hit Coleen if he fired but, in that instant, any jerk or sudden movement from Coleen would pull the knife across Alice's throat. He looked at the gun in his hand. How many rounds were left? He had fired two into Patrick. Patrick had fired one at him, one into the air and at least one more from the signal box. It was a Webley MkV, they carried six rounds. It only needed Patrick to have fired one more round that he did not know about and the gun was empty.

He turned his attention back to Coleen his mind made up.

'I'll throw the gun away but if you don't let her go, I'll rip your throat out with my bare hands.'

'Throw it pretty boy.'

Wath tossed the pistol back towards Patricks body. Street lamps were starting to come on and by their light behind her he could see Lucy entering the churchyard. He turned back to Coleen.

'Let her go.'

Coleen relaxed her grip on Alice, the girl ripped herself away and started running past Wath. He watched her go, she raced past the body and into Lucy's arms. They stood in the middle of the graves hugging each other tightly. He turned his attention back to Coleen.

Too late.

She threw herself at him stabbing with the knife. He tried to move but was slow. The knife entered his shoulder and stabbed through. Coleen ripped it back out, tearing flesh, screaming as she did. Wath staggered but was expecting the next attack.

She stabbed again and he raised his left hand. Piecing his palm, the blade slid through the fleshy middle of his hand and Wath closed his fingers around the cross handle. He punched Coleen with his right hand and yanked the knife from her. She leapt on him scratching, grabbing his hair, trying to find his eyes. He pushed her back and pulled the knife from his hand.

205

She jumped on him again and he tried to push her back again but their legs tangled and they both fell. They landed on top of Abel's grave. Wath was the first to recover and leapt on top of Coleen. He placed his left hand around her throat, blood streaming from the hole in his palm.

He jabbed the knife into her chest, his face inches from hers and looked into her eyes.

'Goodbye Coleen.'

Pressing on the knife he felt it push through her chest into her heart. He stared into her eyes, watching. They glared furiously then subsided, pain shot through them and they started to glaze. As they did the pupils opened wide and Wath stared into a venomous pit.

Compassionless, cruel, cold hearted, devoid of mercy.

A flicker, then Coleen was gone.

He rolled off her and staggered to his feet. He limped towards Lucy. He could see Henry entering the churchyard behind her. He stumbled then slipped, crashing to the grass he realised he had slipped on his own blood. He turned over onto his back and closed his eyes.

Sleep came ever so quickly and easily.

He must have slept for a long time because when he woke the sun was up.

The churchyard was covered in meadow grass and daisies and dandelions and buttercups and corn flowers. And poppies, lots of poppies. It was morning, he needed to get on with his deliveries but there was a mist. It was a low mist covering the field. Wath sat up to be above the haze and the sun was glorious, its wonderful heat burning off the low lying, grey-white vapour.

As he started to get to his feet, he realised it wasn't a mist. It was ghosts. Hundreds and hundreds of ghosts all lying on the ground. They were all men. Men he'd killed. Men who died alongside him. Men he didn't know. Men he did. Men who marched out of England with him. Men who marched from Germany to meet him. Hundreds and hundreds of them and they were all looking at him asking why he was not yet dead.

But the sun was a furnace and the haze started to clear. One by one the shapes faded until they vanished. There was a hollow where the mist was dark and treacle thick. Slowly the figures evaporated until the only shape left was in the hollow. The shape stood up and took on the form of a man. He was tall and unyielding.

There was a noose around his neck.

He began to fade and as he did, he turned away from Wath and started to walk. He looked back over his shoulder and raised his arm. He pointed and curled his finger in the classic come with me gesture. He took two more paces before he evaporated into thin air.

All that was left was meadow grass, daisies, buttercups, dandelions, corn flowers and poppies.

Wath looked up into the sky, it was cobalt blue with not a cloud in sight. He turned his eyes towards the sun. It was speaking. It spoke with Lucy's voice

'Wath, wake up Wath.'

It was glowing bright and at its side hanging in the clear blue sky was the moon except it wasn't the moon and it wasn't still. It was a bullet and it was spinning and coming towards him, straight for him, he knew it had his name. He could read it and his name was coming and coming, getting larger and larger, closer and…

'Wath for God's sake wake up.'

'Wath.'

'Come on man wake up.'

'Wath.'

'WATH!'

Thank you for reading Treacle Town.

This novel is fiction. All the characters are the work of my imagination.

But Treacle Town existed - as described.

Other books written by Leigh Dyson and available on Amazon.

The Magpie Barks

As a young girl in Newcastle tragedy strikes for Margaret and life spirals until the family are forced to flee. They land in Top Yard, Packman Road, West Melton, a small Yorkshire mining village. Two rows of terraced houses forming a triangle around a patch of mud bordering a flooded brickyard quarry.

Here Margaret finds love and security with Gilbert and their adopted daughter, Eva. But as World War Two breaks out old ghosts resurface and when the blitz starts, they uncover a plot to assist the bombing of Sheffield.

In a page turning thriller, they are forced to decide - are they seeking revenge or saving lives.

"Brilliant": **C Law**

"I simply love this book": **Sue W**

"Wow! What a bombshell": **PB**

Treacle Town

It's the address no one aspires to.
Treacle Town.

It's the start in life no one needs.
Abandoned at birth.
Given away as a baby.

It's the cv no one employs.
Taught to thieve as a child.
Trained to kill as a youth.

It's the reputation no one wants.
The Devil's Whelp.

But when you live with it you have to limit your ambition.
Or do you?

A fast-paced thriller set in Wath upon Dearne in 1920 when
unemployment is rife, Spanish Flu rages, Irish Independence flares and
industrial unrest simmers. In post war England dreams are for everyone
but opportunity is only for the privileged.

"Gripping Stuff – loved it":   **A Foster**

"A brilliant read, it's a page turner": **A Bourne**

*"This is an outstanding, can't put down, want more
book.":*   **Kerry**

Cuckoo Crossing

It's 1817 and the richest man in England, Lord Wentworth - the Earl of Malton, is dying from wounds inflicted two years previously during the Napoleonic Wars. The Earl's butler, Kenworthy, is managing the fabulously wealthy estate during the Earls long enfeeblement. He employs Quade, a Scot from Sunderland's highlands estate as gamekeeper. Suddenly Quade is struggling to maintain his personal moral code as events around him become ever more sinister.

The Earl's next of kin, his cousin Lord Sunderland, and the Earl's wife, Lady Charlotte, dislike each other intensely. Both want the estate. Both want to see the other impoverished.

Only one can succeed and Quade is the man in the middle.

"Really enjoyed": **Phil**

"His best yet!": **J Moore**

"Brilliant read from start to finish... didn't want the book to end.": **Jackie R**

Sister Hildræd

It's one thousand and seventy years since the death of our Lord and the Invader is crushing rebellions in the north of England by laying waste to the land, murdering the inhabitants and destroying their livestock.

A boy nearing manhood is caught up in the maelstrom. He meets Sister Hildræd a nun who has visions. A nun instructed by God to take revenge.

They embark upon a journey which will test her faith and his loyalty.

A journey which will become legend.

Be the first to post a review!

Printed in Great Britain
by Amazon

24964465R00119